# ANITA SHREVE

NATIONAL
BESTSELLER

"Fascinating....A slender novel
with a large and complex subject."
—*Washington Post*

## *Stella Bain*

By the author of *Rescue* and *The Pilot's Wife*

# Praise for Anita Shreve's
# *Stella Bain*

"From the opening pages, Shreve writes with a spare directness and quiet urgency about aspects of life during World War I. The descriptions of Stella's time in the field and hospital in France are especially compelling—touching, heartbreaking, sometimes so vivid you can almost feel the fear and smell the stench of death and decay. She delves insightfully into the nature of trauma, shell shock, and memory loss. But the novel is most effective in the small personal moments, as she traces one woman's journey to recover her memory, renegotiate past relationships, forge new connections, and embrace life anew." —Karen Campbell, *Boston Globe*

"Shreve's spare, elegant novel unravels the mysterious past of a wounded army nurse in World War I....Stella's pursuit of truth reveals the bitter sacrifices she has made to survive....Shreve's fans will appreciate her keen understanding of women's struggles to live life on their own terms." —Helen Rogan, *People*

"An intriguing character study that delivers compelling mystery without melodrama. Shreve offers a fresh, feminine twist on a topic that's much in vogue lately—World War I....Shreve cleverly and movingly shifts between Stella's two lives as we learn who she really is. A custody battle, a horrible case of wartime disfigurement, and even questions of women's rights emerge in this spare but involving novel." —Jocelyn McClurg, *USA Today*

"The gripping, touching tale of a shell-shocked American in post–WWI London." —*Good Housekeeping*

"Harrowing.... With the story of this one woman, Shreve gives shape to the larger world of the Great War, presenting an era resonant with heartbreak and with countless acts of valor amid inconceivable suffering.... Shreve infuses *Stella Bain* with warmth and intelligence.... Her writing creates an atmosphere you long to immerse yourself in, one that is filled with interesting, distinctive characters you want to learn more about. I found myself looking forward to the end of the day, when I could again pick up the book and return to this time and these people."     —Carol Iaciofano, NPR

"A slender novel with a large and complex subject.... Shreve examines what shell shock meant in the early twentieth century and how women's injuries were ignored or misinterpreted. And she provides a fascinating portrayal of early Freudian psychiatric treatment and early plastic surgery.... Shreve creates a good-sized canvas of intelligent, well-meaning, well-educated human beings trying to adjust their longings to the rough wishes of the larger world at war."     —Carolyn See, *Washington Post*

"A sweeping saga of World War I.... As Stella's health improves, her astonishing back story is slowly revealed—and it's one that twists and turns in brilliant and unexpected ways. Shreve is a versatile writer, depicting the brutality of battle just as compellingly as she does the early stages of love. She had me rooting for Stella's happiness the whole way through and left me completely satisfied at the end."     —Diana Colvard, *Real Simple*

"Stella's journey of self-discovery allows us to encounter the horrors of the first World War, groundbreaking treatments in psychotherapy, early acknowledgments of domestic violence, and the glimmer of first-wave feminism." —Alice Short, *Los Angeles Times*

"The most vivid prose and emotionally resonant moments come in the middle of the novel, when we flash back and learn the details of the past, and Stella's true name.... The true power of *Stella Bain* lies not in what is said, but in what is left unsaid. The silences are complex: silences within relationships and the silences that come from misunderstanding the complicated mental and emotional consequences of war. And though the story is dark, its resolution is hopeful and nostalgic." —Natalie Bakopoulos, *San Francisco Chronicle*

"*Stella Bain* spares no details in its homage to women who had to fight for justice—it's a well-crafted and engrossing story from one of the country's most established novelists.... Stella is a talented, independent woman ahead of her time, and Shreve maintains the tension as Stella wages a legal battle, establishes her career and regains a family." —Cheryl Krocker McKeon, *Shelf Awareness*

"A tragic yet hopeful story of love, memory, loss, and rebuilding.... Shreve's thoughtful, provocative historical tale has modern resonance." —*Publishers Weekly*

"A compulsively readable novel.... She can evoke an intense feeling in just a few words.... She also grapples with questions that preoccupy women still; where is the balance in seeking personal happiness separate from the role of a wife and mother? How far is one obliged to go to right a wrong; and what price do those dearest to us demand when we keep some part of us solely to ourselves?" —Laura Eggertson, *Toronto Star*

"An exemplary addition to Shreve's already impressive oeuvre. ... The characters are well drawn and sympathetic. Many surprises are in store." —*Kirkus Reviews*

ALSO BY ANITA SHREVE

*Rescue*

*A Change in Altitude*

*Testimony*

*Body Surfing*

*A Wedding in December*

*Light on Snow*

*All He Ever Wanted*

*Sea Glass*

*The Last Time They Met*

*Fortune's Rocks*

*The Pilot's Wife*

*The Weight of Water*

*Resistance*

*Where or When*

*Strange Fits of Passion*

*Eden Close*

# Stella Bain

A NOVEL

## ANITA SHREVE

BACK BAY BOOKS
LITTLE, BROWN AND COMPANY
New York  Boston  London

Copyright © 2013 by Anita Shreve
Reading group guide copyright © 2014 by Anita Shreve and Little, Brown and Company

Back Bay Books / Little, Brown and Company
Hachette Book Group
237 Park Avenue, New York, NY 10017
littlebrown.com

Originally published in hardcover by Little, Brown and Company, November 2013
First Back Bay paperback edition May 2014

Back Bay Books is an imprint of Little, Brown and Company. The Back Bay Books name and logo are trademarks of Hachette Book Group, Inc.

The publisher is not responsible for websites (or their content) that are not owned by the publisher.

The Hachette Speakers Bureau provides a wide range of authors for speaking events. To find out more, go to hachettespeakersbureau.com or call (866) 376-6591.

Library of Congress Cataloging-in-Publication Data
Shreve, Anita.
Stella Bain / Anita Shreve.—First Edition.
pages cm.
ISBN 978-0-316-09886-1 (hardcover) / ISBN 978-0-316-09885-4 (large print) /
ISBN 978-0-316-09889-2 (pb)
1. World War, 1939–1945—Fiction. 2. War neuroses—Fiction. I. Title.
PS3569.H7385S57 2013
813'.54—dc23
2013025618

10 9 8 7 6 5 4 3 2 1

RRD-C

Printed in the United States of America

*For Asya*

*Marne, March 1916*

Sunrise glow through canvas panels. Foul smell of gas gangrene. Men moaning all around her. Pandemonium and chaos.

She floats inside a cloud. Cottony, a little dingy. Pinpricks of light summon her to wakefulness. She drifts, and then she sleeps.

Distinct sounds of metal on metal, used instruments tossed into a pan. She tries to remember why she lies on a cot, enclosed within panels of canvas, a place where men who die are prepared for burial away from the rest of the wounded, a task she has performed any number of times.

She glances down and finds that she is wearing mauve men's pajamas. Why do her feet hurt?

A small piece of cloth with a question mark on it is pinned to a uniform hanging from a hook. For several minutes, she studies the uniform before realizing that she does not know her own name. She receives this fact with growing anxiety.

The name *Lis* floats lightly into her thoughts. But she does not think Lis is her name. Elizabeth...? No. Ella...? Ellen...? Possibly, though there ought to be a sibilant. She ponders the empty space where a name should be.

\*   \*   \*

The name *Stella* bubbles up into her consciousness. Can Stella be it? She examines the letters as they appear in her mind, and the more she studies them, the more certain she is that Stella is correct.

Again, she drifts into a half sleep. When she comes to, she cannot remember the name she has decided upon. She lets her mind empty, and, gradually, it returns.
*Stella.*
Such a small thing.
Such a big thing.

Stella has no idea where she has come from. She senses it might be an unhappy place, a door she might not want to open. But no one's entire past can be unhappy, can it? It might contain unhappy events or a tendency toward melancholy, but the whole cannot be miserable.

All around her, the hum of flies and the beat of fast footsteps. Orders are shouted; a new batch of wounded is coming in; the staff will want her bed, of course they will. There is nothing wrong with her, and she has simply been allowed to sleep a long time.

She rubs her feet together. A sharp pain through the muffling of bandages. How has she injured her feet?

A panel is moved aside, and she hears a woman speak in French. Seconds later, a nurse, a nun, enters the small canvas compartment. As she moves toward the bed, she looms large in her starched uniform and wimple. She scrutinizes Stella's eyes, scanning, the patient knows, for dilated pupils. "You are British?" the sister asks.

"I am not sure," Stella answers.

"You have been unconscious for two days," the sister explains, stepping back and fussing with the sheets as she slides Stella's feet from under the covers. "Your feet had bits of shrapnel in them when you arrived. Someone with a cart left you outside the tent in the middle of the night. I should like to examine your feet."

This is someone else's story, Stella thinks, not hers.

"What is your name?"

"Stella." She pauses. "Where am I?"

"Marne."

"Marne is in France?"

"Yes," the sister answers, pursing her mouth. "My name is Sister Luke. I am British, but almost everyone else at the camp is French. We believe your boots blew off when you were knocked unconscious by the first shell and that a second shell injured your feet. You had not a scratch on you otherwise, apart from some bruises from falling."

"Will I be able to walk?" Stella asks.

Sister Luke studies her. "I think you are American."

"Am I?"

"From your accent. But you were found in a British VAD uniform."

Stella cannot explain this.

"You are a VAD?"

"I don't know."

Stella can see that the sister is annoyed and has other, more pressing matters to attend to.

"But I know how to drive an ambulance," she blurts out.

Is this true? If not, why does she think it is?

"You know this, and yet you do not know your posting?" the sister asks with barely concealed disbelief.

Yes, the paradox is bewildering but does not seem urgent. Beyond the canvas, Stella knows, everything is urgent.

The sister moves toward the opening in the compartment. "Apart from your feet, I can find nothing wrong with you. You will have them examined and dressed on a regular basis. Then you will rest and eat and drink while we ascertain your identification. We will contact all the nearby hospital camps. You cannot have come very far. When your feet are better, you can work. Perhaps we will see if you can drive that ambulance after all. In the meantime, you are to remain here. What is your last name?"

Stella simply shakes her head.

Orders are given, and a nurse's aide arrives with a tray. The dressing of Stella's wounds is more painful than she would have thought possible. The aide, who looks exhausted, helps Stella drink two glasses of water. Stella feels sorry for the young woman and does not ask questions because she knows the effort it will take to answer them.

Stella's last name comes to her the way a bird takes flight. She tells the aide, "I am Stella Bain."

\*　　\*　　\*

When the aide leaves, Stella closes her eyes and then opens them. She repeats this exercise several times. But no matter how often she does it, she cannot remember what regiment she was attached to or what she was doing on a battlefield.

A month later, Stella has recovered from her wounds and serves as a nurse's aide in a French uniform. Again, she puzzles over the way her skills have returned to her, even though she does not know where she learned them.

Stella is appalled by her surroundings: the soil thick with manure; mud-laced wounds causing suppurating infections; compound fractures imposing a death sentence. A swab of Lysol along with gauze dipped in iodine is all the medicine on offer. A gas-gangrenous wound, not to be confused with the effect of poisoned gas, balloons up to grotesque proportions. Stella watches a doctor play an idle beat upon a man's flesh with his fingers. The sight is awful, the sound hollow. Almost all the men die.

Sometimes, the doctors' screams are louder than the patients'. The surgeon's job is beyond belief, a hell on earth worse than any hell imagined. Stella wants to know how many of them go mad, all sensibility and religion violently stripped away during the endless succession of amputations.

Always look a man in the eye, no matter how terrible the wound. This the English sister teaches, orders, her to do. The wounded's journey is long: from the trenches of no-man's-land to the aid post to the field dressing station to the casualty-clearing station, only to die on the train on the way to the base hospital.

*     *     *

In her off-hours, Stella mends tears in her skirt, brushes mud off her hem, and searches for lice in the seams of her clothing. She washes collars and cuffs and the cloth of her cap, and if there is water left over, she tries to clean her body.

One day, she asks the sister on duty if she might have a piece of paper and a pencil. In her tent, Stella begins to sketch what she can see around her: a lantern, a canvas table, a cot in the corner. Her roommate, Jeanne, catches her at this activity and marvels at Stella's ability. In broken English and using a kind of sign language, she asks if Stella will draw her portrait so that she might send it back to her family. Jeanne has hollow eyes and a vocation. As she draws the young woman, Stella wants to ask her how her religion has survived the sights they have both witnessed, but Stella's grasp of French is not good enough for any sort of meaningful conversation.

When Jeanne brings a fellow aide to the tent and asks Stella if she will draw her friend's portrait, Stella agrees on the condition that Jeanne find her more paper and pencils and a knife for sharpening the pencils. This Jeanne happily does. Jeanne's friend insists on paying Stella for her sketch. Gradually, a number of nurses and their aides line up to have their portraits done as well.

But between the portraits, when Stella is alone, the private drawings she makes disturb her. She sketches the exteriors of unknown houses, surrounded by grotesque trees and bushes. When she tries again, the drawings are nearly the same, but the atmosphere of claustrophobia grows even more pronounced. The sketches produce a keen sense of distress, but she cannot stop herself from continuing to make them.

Stella does not know how she came by her skill at drawing. It seems to have appeared simply out of a desire to do so.

The English sister must have remembered Stella's statement that she can drive an ambulance, for she receives her first assignment on a June night.

"Over and up," the French orderly beside her says. The ambulance bucks, but does not stall. Stella has to feel her way along the road, since no lights can be used. Her eyes strain and water. In the distance, rockets throw a greenish light over the countryside.

Stella screams when a shell bursts two hundred feet ahead. First, a large splash of earth, and then a ball of smoke, which drifts away. The orderly swears, French words that she understands. The orderly is fluent in English, which is, Stella supposes, the reason he has been assigned to her.

"It's going to get rough," the man explains. "Especially when we pull in. That is where we are most vulnerable. As soon as I jump off, you turn the truck around and keep the engine running. Someone will help me load. When I pound the back here, you start driving, no matter what is happening. You find a way to get back."

Physical fear begins to climb Stella's spine, and yet she has done this before, has she not? Her hand shakes on the gearshift. She squeezes her shoulder blades together, expecting a direct hit to the Croix Rouge symbol on the roof. She has no idea where the road begins. She struggles to see the slightest indication of tracks, but smoke clouds the path. How will she find her way back to camp with the wounded inside? Regulations prohibit her from stopping at any point, even if the men behind her start to shout.

She senses the bump of each stretcher as it is loaded into the back of the bus. She waits for the pounding on the wooden panel.

Stella does not know how many are in the back, how badly wounded they are. She cannot even be sure it is the orderly himself who has signaled to her. She wishes he were up front so that she could talk to him.

"Left," she says aloud to herself as she finds and follows the tracks. And later, "Slow down."

When she arrives back at camp, she slides like a reptile from the driver's seat. Despite the cold, she has perspired through to her coat. She counts the wounded as they are unloaded. She is struck by their apparent freedom from pain. Stranger still, she can hear one of them whistling. She feels stronger and lighter than she has in months.

One day, walking through the camp, Stella hears a man curse the institution that assigned his brother to a ship that sank. Her mind snags on the word *Admiralty* in the sentence. She puzzles over it so much in the days that follow that *Admiralty* becomes a kind of mythic goal, a monolith drawing her toward it. She believes that she will one day reach it, and she hopes that once she sees the building or the landscape, she will remember why it seems to be so important. But how strange, because to her knowledge she has never been in England. Can her quest be the result of an event in her former life?

*Admiralty* hums in its own layer, the one behind the present moment and before the void that is her memory. A word. A title.

A note. It presses and troubles her, even when she actively tries to think of something else.

Stella learns that the Admiralty, headquarters to the British Royal Navy, stands in central London. She begins to cherish the word because she believes it comes from her previous life, perhaps the first chink in the armor of her inner mind, where memory and identity lie. Has she ever worked at the Admiralty? Lived close to it? Did she once have a husband who worked there? The notion threatens her, because she cannot imagine having forgotten something as basic as a man she loved and the intimacy they shared. Often she studies her fingers, searching for a tiny circle that might signal the previous presence of a wedding band. But she has found nothing. In the privacy of her tent, shortly after her arrival, she conducted a physical examination. A husband or a lover is a possibility.

Throughout the summer, Stella's life consists of tending to the wounded, driving an ambulance, and drawing on paper with a pencil. In this way, she sometimes forgets that she cannot remember.

In October, Stella is granted leave. She thinks this might be her one chance to get to England. She must find the Admiralty and discover its importance. Jeanne tells her she should go to Paris.

Stella asks for and is given a canvas satchel in which she packs her British uniform, her sketches, and the money she has earned from making portraits of nurses and their aides.

Once in Paris, she catches a train for the coast, where, she has heard, English hospital ships carrying wounded men are setting out for home. But the train, due to heavy bombardment, has to stop before it reaches Étaples. Even from a distance of ten miles, the shelling can be heard. The hospital personnel are urged to stay in their seats; the train will be rerouted.

With her satchel, Stella slips from the train and makes her way into the woods. If her exit has been seen, will they bother to look for her? She cannot imagine a doctor or a train conductor trying to find her. Stella remains, for the moment, a stateless woman in a lawless country.

The journey through the forest is arduous and frightening, but gradually the woods thin out to reveal the coastal village. Along the way, she encounters a chaos such as she has never seen before. She begins to cough, whether from the smoke or illness she cannot tell. In Étaples, Stella discovers that the large Red Cross hospital ship to which the wounded were headed has partially sunk.

She ducks inside a tent and changes into her British VAD uniform. "I've lost my way," she tells the first official-looking British man she meets.

"They're using smaller ships now to get across the Channel. There's a dock at the eastern end you might try."

Stella locates a ship that was perhaps a ferry or a pleasure boat. There is no pleasure aboard it now. When she sees the cargo, she gasps. The wounded and the dead have not been separated. The calls of the injured sound as if they come from an underworld she has only dreamed about. Here and there, she observes nurse's aides like herself comforting men and applying dressings.

No one asks to see her identity card. No one cares. She does what she has been doing for months in Marne, tending to the wounded and assisting with operations that cannot wait until they reach the shore.

When in England, Stella boards a train with the most seriously hurt, the ones who might not, even with a doctor's ministrations, make it to Victoria station. En route, the men are sick and their bowels loosen. There is a priest on board to deliver last rites, and it is one of Stella's duties to make sure she can find the man at any given moment.

In London, Stella silently wishes the wounded well and then leaves them. Trading with the soldiers heading toward the front, she exchanges her French money for English money. Exhausted, Stella follows a crowd along what looks to be a main thoroughfare. She walks in a direction she thinks will lead to the Admiralty, but after a while senses that she has made a mistake. Finding herself on a narrow lane, she tries to retrace her steps. She walks without food or water, fingering the unfamiliar British coins inside her pocket. She moves forward until she can walk no more, but still she keeps trudging. She walks until she comes to a stop against a wrought-iron fence. A woman in a rose-colored suit asks her a question.

*London, October 1916*

A woman in a rose-colored suit, which strikes Stella as both odd and beautiful because she has seen little color on anyone in London, asks her if she is unwell.

"My name is Lily Bridge. From my window across the garden, I saw you leaning against the fence. Pardon my candor, but you seem to be overwrought."

Who, Stella would like to know, is not overwrought in this time and place?

Stella can barely lift herself upright. All of life, it seems, resembles static from a radio, full of people and words and smells, if only she could sort out the frequencies. Sometimes the confusion taxes her intellect, as if it were a problem she had to solve. At other times, it is a soft cocoon that comforts her.

"Will you walk over to our house and come inside and sit for a minute?" Lily asks. "It's quite raw out here."

Stella does not want to give herself over to another, but at the moment, she is not sure she will even make it to the woman's front door.

Lily takes Stella's arm. Stella coughs deeply and is rattled by a searing pain in her chest. After she steps inside, a butler takes her cloak and gloves and satchel. Lily urges her toward a fire in a large, welcoming room. In the warmth, Stella becomes aware of the awful stench that wafts from her. It is, she knows, the smell of French muck, of men's leaking wounds, and of fear. She has not washed in two days.

Stella cannot remember the last time she stood in someone's house. The shiny red tiles of the fireplace surround, the mantel with its diamond-paned frieze below the shelf, and the tulip chandelier intrigue her. Many volumes have been pressed together on the shelves of a bookcase.

Stella cannot sit, as she has been asked to do, on the striped red silk settee. She wants no part of her filthy uniform to touch the pristine surroundings. When Lily insists, however, Stella lowers herself to the edge of a paisley wing chair. Lily, who seems attentive to her mood, murmurs soothing words from time to time.

A man comes through the front door, bringing with him the bluster of the weather and an air of affability. "I've come to tell you that I'll be late tonight," he says, addressing Lily. "Oh, I'm sorry. I didn't know you had a guest." He gives his hat and coat to the butler, whom he calls Streeter.

"August, this woman is a VAD," Lily explains. "I found her quite exhausted, and I invited her to sit for a moment."

"Yes, of course," says the man, who studies Stella.

In turn, she notices a tall tuft of dark hair, a clean-shaven face, navy eyes inside silver spectacles. She senses a strong intelligence.

The butler returns with a tray of biscuits, cheese, and apple slices as well as a large pot of tea. Stella takes her cup and holds it with both hands, not trusting herself not to drop it. An odd quiet descends. It is the silence of embarrassment, apprehension, and ordinary kindness.

"My name is Stella Bain," she announces after a time. "As you must have guessed, I am an American."

* * *

Lily persuades Stella to go upstairs and lie down. As Stella follows Iris, Lily's maid, she hears Lily, on the bottom step, speaking in a low voice to her husband in the hallway. "I think she isn't at all well."

"I agree. I'll telephone Michael Fain straightaway."

Lily shows Stella her bedroom. In it, she waits for the maid to draw her a bath.

"You can sleep here," Lily says.

"You are very kind."

Stella is used to being told what to do. In any case, there is no thought of doing otherwise. After her bath, she changes into her nightgown and slips between the sheets. She drifts off, but is woken often during the night by her worsening cough.


Dr. Fain makes several visits, alarmed by Stella's rising fever. She is aware of a genial man whose hair might once have been blond and who wears golden spectacles. She is unused to doctors who have the time to perform proper examinations, to talk to their patients, and even, occasionally, to smile.

The doctor prescribes medicine, but Stella does not seem to get any better. Feverish, she soaks her sheets at night and sits outside her room while the maid changes them. Lily, in her dressing gown, stands near Stella, sometimes resting a hand on her shoulder.

Stella drinks hot bouillon and cool water. On the fifth night, there is an unexpected crisis, and Dr. Fain is summoned to the home. Stella's fever is dangerously high, and she is having trouble breathing. Lily, the doctor, and Iris take turns sitting with Stella during the night. She hallucinates a fire and tries to climb out of bed. Her head aches nearly all the time. She sweats and shivers and coughs so much her throat hurts.

When she is alone with Dr. Fain, she asks him his diagnosis. He hesitates, knowing that she is a nurse's aide and will understand the gravity of the pronouncement. "Pneumonia, I think," he says quietly.

"I thought as much," Stella replies, turning her face away.

Her recovery is both agonizingly slow and remarkable. As her cough eases up, her temperature gradually returns to normal. Lily brings fattening lunches to Stella's room and often stays to eat with her. They make pleasant conversation. Stella learns that Lily is originally from Greenwich, that she and August have been married eight years, and that she volunteers at a settlement house three days a week. Stella is surprised to discover that Lily's husband is also a doctor, a cranial surgeon with a clinic in Harley Street.

"He works all the hours of the day," Lily says, perhaps offering a subtle apology for why he has not visited Stella. She is surprised that he did not once come to see how she was faring.

Lily is petite, with coloring opposite from Stella's. Whereas Stella has acorn-colored hair and golden brown eyes, Lily is blond, with light blue eyes. She dresses well, but not extravagantly—a nod to the war, Stella suspects.

On the eleventh day, Stella opens the velvet drapery to sunshine. She feels better than she has in weeks. In the mahogany wardrobe, she finds, in addition to her uniform, two dresses tailored in the style of the uniform. One is navy wool with silver embroidery on the collar; the other is the color of tea with milk.

She is to make a decision then. If she chooses the uniform, the garment will announce, once she descends the stairs, her intention to leave the house. If she picks either the navy or fawn dress, she will be signaling that she will stay, even though she has not been formally invited to do so. With some reluctance—she wants nothing more than to return to the bed—she puts on the uniform, appreciating its cleanliness.

Stella does not want to leave the room. Apart from its comforts, which are many—the bed with its ironed sheets, the enormous bath and warm towels, the pretty arrangement of boudoir chairs nestled in front of the tall window—she knows that to open the door is to reenter the world as she knew it just eleven days ago, the world of battlefields and guns and shrapnel and dead and dying bodies. She has nearly as much fear of leaving the bedchamber this late October morning as she might have of entering a ward of grotesquely injured men while deafening German shells pound the earth.

Lily, who is waiting for Stella at the bottom of the stairs, holds her smile even though Stella is in uniform. "You are intending to leave us," she pronounces.

"I find I must."

Lily, flustered, backs up as Stella descends the stairs.

"My gratitude toward you and your husband is immense," Stella says. "I can never thank you enough, though I hope you will allow me to pay for my care."

Stella opens her satchel, but Lily waves her hand away. "Nonsense," she says. "I'd have done the same for anyone in your condition."

Stella reluctantly closes her satchel and sets it by her feet.

"August will be home in ten minutes for the luncheon. He'll be upset with me if I have let you go. Besides, you cannot leave without some nourishment."

Stella does not mean to seem formidable or ungracious; Lily is a lovely woman. Stella has no way of knowing whether she was ever a lovely woman herself.

"The clothes in the wardrobe," Stella says. "Did you have them made for me?"

"Yes, I did," Lily says. "You must at least take those. They won't fit anyone else."

"I will do that, then. Thank you."

Stella must find the Admiralty, and she does not want to waste another minute. But equally, she understands that she cannot refuse the woman who has taken such good care of her. "I will stay to eat," she says. "But I should like to take a breath of fresh air first, if I may. Perhaps I could go out to your garden—the public garden in the center of the square."

Lily opens a desk drawer and gives Stella the key.

Stella makes it as far as the nearest bench, the gate quivering behind her. Just inside the tall iron fence, a thinning box hedge echoes the garden's rectangular shape. Pink town houses and a few cream-colored mansions surround the garden. Pollarded plane trees thrust upward from the ground, reminding her of arms with fists.

The air, though cool, is exhilarating. She admires a bed of late-blooming bronze roses, then later a tree, the leaves of which have done a delicate turn from pale green to gold. She hears a motorcar on an adjacent street, somewhere the rasp of coal down a chute.

"Good morning," Dr. Bridge says as he approaches her from the gate. "I've just been home. I understand you plan to leave us."

"Hello," she says. "I am to stay to luncheon and then I must go. You and your wife have been more than generous."

"Where exactly *will* you go?"

"I have an appointment at the Admiralty," she says quietly.

"Indeed? You've said nothing about this. Well, not that I know of."

As he is speaking, the gate clangs open again. Three children and their nanny enter. Though Stella can see Dr. Bridge speaking and even gesturing, suddenly she cannot hear his voice. Despite this, Stella feels calm as she watches the children, all under the age of ten, crisscross the lawn in a game she does not understand.

The nanny sits and waves at her charges, but she looks, with her drawn face and slouch, worn and frayed. From time to time, a girl disappears into the evergreen bushes, later to emerge triumphant. All the anxiety Stella has felt since arriving in London disappears, and it is as though she inhabits a cocoon of warmth and light.

It is only when the children go off with their nanny that sound startles Stella: shifting leaves, motorcars, horses' hooves on pavement, men in conversation, a woman raising her voice. She does not question the disappearance and appearance of her hearing, since this is not the first time it has happened.

"I think we'd better go back to the house," Dr. Bridge says, looking at her oddly.

*     *     *

A fire has been laid adjacent to a round walnut dining table. Stella notices that two places have been set. In a sapphire-blue day dress, Lily gestures for Stella to sit, but she is confused. Where is the third place?

"I have to return to the settlement house," Lily says, answering Stella's unspoken question.

"I hope they won't keep you too long," Dr. Bridge says. "For once I should be on time for dinner tonight."

"Are you uncomfortable?" Dr. Bridge asks when Stella has settled into her chair. Like many surgeons Stella has known, he is a man to get straight to the point.

"Yes and no," she answers as Streeter enters with bowls of what he announces is oxtail soup. "I am grateful for your hospitality. But I worry that I am using up your valuable time at the clinic."

"The clinic is well staffed. We have patients suffering from intense though as yet undiagnosed head pain remaining for observation, while others, recovering from cranial surgery, recuperate." The butler offers them both bread and butter. Dr. Bridge eats like a man who knows to the precise minute how much time he has left to finish his meal. Stella has seen this among men and women at the front.

"Yesterday," he says, "I had a particularly challenging case. An officer with the British Expeditionary Force was sent to my clinic directly after his stay at the Royal Victoria Hospital. His lower mandible had been shot away, and some attempt at crude reconstruction had been made. I assume you have seen similar cases."

He is trying to put them on an equal footing—professional to semiprofessional—another kindness Stella much appreciates, but his anecdote tightens her stomach. "I never saw the reconstruction," she says, picking up her spoon.

"Where were you exactly?"

"Just before my leave, I was billeted at Marne with the French infantry. You were speaking of your patient?"

Dr. Bridge is not an unhandsome man, and she puts him in his late thirties. Though he is careful in his dress and his speech, she senses an ebullience kept tightly bound, as if he had reluctantly left his youth behind.

"When the patient arrived, his lower jaw was badly infected, and I could see that to save the man, the reconstruction would have to be cut away, the infected tissue abraded, and a recovery period endured before we could implant a better device for him. When the officer received this news, he had to be restrained. Having already survived one painful surgery, he was understandably unhappy at the notion of undoing that work, having to live with the misery of saliva constantly dripping from his open wound, and going through all that surgery again. Do these details upset you?"

"Not at all," she says. "Though I am sympathetic."

"The patient began to shout and flail, and I wondered for a moment if his mind hadn't been permanently affected as well."

"I have seen men whose minds have been severely affected by combat."

"Have you?" Dr. Bridge asks, staring intently at Stella.

Streeter removes the bowls and sets down pear salads. As they wait for him to leave, Stella finds herself intrigued by a portrait on the wall of a woman who clearly is not Lily.

"My mother," Dr. Bridge says, noting Stella's gaze. "This was her house, which I inherited upon her death. It's too big for us, really. We are lucky to have Streeter. He injured his leg early in the war, poor man. We have Iris, whom you've met, and Mrs. Ryan, our cook, and Mary Dodsworth, who is our chauffeur. Her husband, Robert, used to drive the Austin before he went to the front. We only use the motorcar when going any distance. In these times of scarcity, we lend it to friends who have necessary errands. Indeed..." He pauses. "I have often been called upon to tend to a wife or a father who has had the worst possible news."

The car has been used for funerals. Stella hopes there has been a wedding or two as well.

The doctor sets his bowl aside. Stella picks up her fork. To her knowledge, she has never eaten pears, and she savors each slice. A faint smell of fish cooking in a pan drifts into the dining room.

"I signed up to go to France," the doctor says, "but I was disqualified because of scoliosis and abysmal eyesight. The fact that my spine doesn't bother me one bit or that my sight is easily corrected did not, I'm afraid, budge the board. 'We need you here, too,' they said by way of consolation." The doctor looks off as if still angry.

"That must have been difficult for you," Stella offers.

"And later, when it became clear that Englishmen were being slaughtered across the Channel and replacements were needed, I tried again, and again I was refused. I have contented myself with treating some of the most severe head wounds that return by hospital ship. I often deal with patients as soon as their trains pull into Waterloo."

"You are doing important work," Stella says.

"No more than any other man." He looks at her. "Or woman."
Stella feels a tingling in her feet.

*Oh, please. God, no.*

She holds her breath a moment, and the tingling subsides.

"You were going to leave us before I even came home?" Dr.
Bridge inquires.

"It was not out of disrespect," Stella says. "I felt it was time to
be on my way. Your wife persuaded me to stay."

He laughs. "She has amazing powers." He smiles to indicate
that these powers are benign and usually put to good purpose.
"Why did you come from America to Europe, and how did
you get here? Perhaps you've talked about this already with
Lily."

"Sometimes it all seems a blur," she answers, half smiling, trying to make the answer seem as casual as possible. Lily *had* asked
her the same question, early on in her stay, and Stella had been
guarded then as well.

"You have a soft voice for someone of your height. You're
nearly as tall as I am. Six feet?"

"Do you always ask your guests such personal questions?" she
asks, again feeling the tingling in her legs.

"Surgeons are rude. I'm sorry. I suppose we think we can get
away with it."

"You have seen dreadful cases."

"As have you. Did you enjoy your war work, however exhaust-
ing?"

"I can't believe anyone enjoys such work, but I did appreciate
the obliteration of thought."

"You were trying to blot out memories."

She shakes her head quickly, a sign to desist, but he presses on.

"I can't help but think," he says, "that someone who tried to get to Europe during a war—a war in which her country wasn't even involved—was either running away from something unpleasant in America or was searching in the most desperate, the most dangerous of ways for the obliteration of self that you speak of."

Stella scoots her chair away from the table and puts her hands on her thighs. She clenches her jaw. Dr. Bridge looks bewildered and stands, but she waves him off with a sudden harsh movement of her hand.

She bends and rubs her legs through the cloth of her skirt, from the tops of her thighs down to her ankles, along the sides of her calves, and up to her thighs again. She is aware that these gestures might be seen as improper, but she is in too much pain to care. Unable to control herself, she utters small, gruff cries. The doctor stands beside her with his hands open.

The pain is unspeakable, and she cannot assuage it no matter how hard she tries. She rubs her legs with increasing frequency and finds it mortifying to be acting in this way in the dining room of a man she barely knows. If she could manage it, she would stand and run out of the house.

"Miss Bain, what is it?"

She is unable to speak for fear of uttering an ugly sound.

"Is the pain terrible? Would morphine help?"

Stella shakes her head.

After a time—fifteen minutes or forty—Stella unclenches her jaw. Her arms tremble, as if she were cold. She wants to be anywhere but in this dining room. The doctor holds her water glass to her lips. After she has taken a sip, she hunches over herself.

"What happened to you just then?" Dr. Bridge asks. That he of all people should have seen the attack is unbearable to Stella, because she knows he will not let it go. But there is no use denying what was perfectly visible. "My legs hurt," she says plainly.

"Do they now?"

"No, the pain is gone."

"Completely gone?"

"Yes."

"Can you describe it?"

For a few minutes, Stella remains silent, and he does not interrupt that silence.

"I have recurring pain in my legs," Stella says finally, "as well as a deafness that is quite real when it happens." She pauses. "Just then it felt as though someone were running a wheel with pins up and down my legs, only the pins were digging deep into my bones."

"I'm so sorry," he says.

She takes a handkerchief from her cuff and blots her face, knowing that her scalp is wet. She has another long sip of water. "I'm embarrassed."

"No need to be. No need at all. It was, I could see, completely beyond your control. The pain looked ghastly. Have you ever broken your legs? Bad fractures can result in lifelong intermittent pain."

She considers how much to tell him. "Seven months ago, I was found unconscious with shrapnel in my feet. The shrapnel was removed, but I had very little infection. It would be tempting to think that was the cause, but most of the time, I haven't any pain and am perfectly able to walk."

"Your feet don't hurt?"

"They did immediately after the surgery to remove the shrapnel, but they healed well."

"Forgive me for my direct questions," the doctor says. "It's mystifying. Do you suffer from arthritis?"

She laughs, feeling giddy as she always does after the cessation of pain. "You think I'm that old?"

"No," he answers, coloring. "Arthritis can affect the very young, as you know. Do episodes such as the one that just occurred happen often?"

"I don't know what 'often' means."

"Once a day? Once a month?"

"It has no schedule."

The tops of her thighs are sore from the rubbing, and she wants nothing more than to lie down. She thinks of excusing herself and going straight up to the room she so recently left.

Dr. Bridge resumes his seat and rests his chin on his hand. The sunlight through the window glints off his spectacles. She is a puzzle to him, one he thinks he ought to be able to solve. She is a puzzle to herself.

"I thought you went deaf in the garden."

"Yes."

The doctor appears to ponder that episode. His roving eyes convey his desire to understand. "Have these occurrences increased in frequency?"

She thinks a minute. "Yes, I suppose they have."

He leans forward, resting his elbows on his knees. "Think back to the moment when you first had the pains in your legs or felt yourself going deaf."

Stella does not like the memory. "I was driving an ambulance from near the front to the hospital camp. I had a sudden and severe pain in my legs, so much so that I had to stop the ambulance, which I had been told never to do. Getting the wounded to the camp was urgent. I didn't know what had happened or how long the duration of the pain would be. At first, I thought I had been hit."

"With a bullet or shrapnel."

"Yes. But when I finally made it back to our camp, I examined myself and could find no blood or wound."

Dr. Bridge considers her answer. "Did you tell anyone about the pain?"

"No."

"No physician examined you? Looked at your legs or feet?"

"No. My only examination happened shortly after I arrived at the camp."

"And the deafness?"

"It happened simultaneously with the legs. It also occurs by itself, though, as it did today in the garden."

Aware that they have been talking in somewhat modulated tones, Stella sits back. Whether consciously or not, Dr. Bridge mimics her posture.

"Why didn't you tell anyone?" he asks. "I assume there were good doctors in Marne."

"I would have been sent to England or back to America," she explains. "Or worse, I would have been stripped of my duties as an ambulance driver. One couldn't have a driver who might at any moment become disabled."

"How did you become an ambulance driver?" he asks.

"Though I worked as a nurse's aide, I was asked to drive an ambulance. I told them I'd done it before."

"Truly?" he says, surprised.

Why has she added that bit of information? To impress him? To show him she is no ordinary VAD?

"Highly unusual, I should think, Miss Bain," he adds.

Stella remains silent.

"Are you all right?" he asks.

For one dizzying moment, Stella thinks the honorific incorrect.

After a pause, Dr. Bridge asks, "May I ask you what drew you to Bryanston Square?"

"Is that where I am?" Stella gazes through the window at the green-gold oasis. She wonders once again how much to tell him. "I need to go to the Admiralty. It feels urgent."

"You're about an hour away on foot. You must have been in great distress to have come straight from the hospital ship and not bother to first find a place to sleep for the night."

Heat rises to her face.

Streeter enters and sets down plates. The fish does not look appetizing, and she doubts that it will be warm.

"In the course of my practice of cranial surgery," Dr. Bridge begins, "I have come upon a number of bizarre physical phenomena. Though I'm a surgeon, I'm intrigued by these odd occurrences and have often sought the advice of other doctors whose knowledge has helped to illuminate a thorny problem of my own."

"Hence your interest in me?"

"My interest in you is humanitarian. If I may, I should like to make a suggestion."

She meets his gaze.

"Even though you have improved tremendously, I think you know you are not entirely well. Do you understand that you cannot go back to France until your symptoms subside?"

"I must go back," she explains. "Otherwise I'll be written down as absent without leave."

"I doubt the penalties for American volunteers are as severe as for the English or French soldier, but I'll investigate."

"No, please don't," she says, then stands. "Thank you for your concern."

"You must finish your lunch," the doctor says. "I believe Mrs. Ryan has gone to the trouble of making a pudding."

Does the doctor imagine she cannot see through his transparent ploy?

The doctor eats in silence, perhaps mindful of the clock. Stella cannot bring herself to touch the fish, the sauce of which has congealed on her plate. After a time, Streeter enters the room to clear the dishes and to bring out a warm bread pudding with custard, a course Stella thinks she can eat.

Dr. Bridge speaks in the voice of a man who has composed his thoughts. "I wish you to stay a few more nights with my wife and me. As you can see, we have plenty of room, and neither I nor Lily would feel comfortable if you left now. In fact, I should feel that I was putting you in harm's way or worse—that if I let you go, you might injure others should your symptoms overcome you at a critical moment."

Stella puts a hand up.

"This isn't to say that you aren't free to go," Dr. Bridge continues. "Of course you are. This is merely my recommendation. If you could but think of this as a temporary rest stop, I believe progress can be made. We can certainly get you back on your feet. We can speak further another time."

He has no idea who I am, she thinks.

*I have no idea who I am.*

Stella stands. "You think, Dr. Bridge, that my most acute problem at the moment is the physical occurrences you have witnessed. But it's not. My greatest difficulty is that I can't remember anything in my life prior to waking in a hospital tent in Marne in March of this year." She moves toward the door. "I appreciate your concern, but I have places I must go. Please thank your wife again. She has been extremely kind."

Streeter appears next to Stella with her cloak and satchel.

"Good-bye, Dr. Bridge," she says.

Gusts of wind blow Stella's skirt about. The clean uniform as well as the decent food she has had to eat lift her spirits. What she needs is a map of London, and she wonders if such things are readily available. In France, a map was a rarity, unless it was a fake. She walks along the street until she sees a boy selling newspapers. She asks if he knows where she can get a map.

"A map of what?"

"Of London. Do you have one for sale?"

"No, miss. Where do you want to go?"

"To the Admiralty."

The boy raises an eyebrow, whether out of respect or fear she is not sure.

"I can draw you how to get there," he suggests.

She watches as he grips the pencil he stores behind his ear with an earnestness that charms her. After a time, he hands her a rudimentary but satisfactory-looking map drawn on a piece of newsprint. She can just make out the letters. She takes some coins out of her pocket, but does not know their precise worth. She hands the boy one of the smaller ones.

"Oh, no, miss, you don't want to give me that. Here's a truth. The larger the coin, the less it's worth. Well, usually. This one here's enough for me."

Stella drops the coin into his palm. She wants to give him an-

36 • Anita Shreve

other, perhaps for the way he held the pencil in his fingers. He is just a boy, no older than twelve. She hopes the war will be over before he can lie about his age to enlist.

Stella follows the street names and makes turns where indicated.

Along the way, she comes upon a stationery shop and enters. She asks for two sheets of writing paper, an envelope, and several pencils. She further inquires if the gentleman behind the counter will sharpen them for her. She is certain that he will do this; her uniform carries weight wherever she goes.

On the map, the boy drew an X at her destination, and from what she can tell, after she has walked another fifteen minutes, she has reached it. She gazes up at a large building.

The Admiralty means nothing to Stella. What did she expect? A tower with pinnacles? Surely not this squat piece of masonry. Magnificent—imposing, even—but not the stuff of myth.

Near the entrance, one-legged men stand, leaning on straight sticks. Others have pinned-up sleeves. Still others sit in wheel-chairs, two trousered stumps for legs. Have they come as she has to this building, not knowing why?

After a few minutes, she understands that they are beggars, hardly any of them making a sound. Those in uniform stand or sit with dignity. Some have mothers or sons by their sides. Stella watches as passersby tuck coins into their hands and pockets, a way of saying, "I am sorry; my son came home intact." Or "With these coins, I bargain; my child is still in France." Do fathers give coins for daughters? A thousand daughters are losing their souls and sometimes their lives abroad. Does anyone think of them? Has she lost her soul? Is that what is missing, what has been taken from her? Is that why she cannot remember?

The noise of the city grates on her nerves. Motorcars and omnibuses, cries for help, orders given, the click of gates. She approaches a guard, and by the way he watches her, she knows that her few steps are too many in his direction. He holds up his hand in the halt position.

"Is it possible to go inside?" she asks.

"Do you have a letter?"

"A letter?"

"Of introduction."

She has no letter of introduction. She does not even have a name. For what reason might a person want to enter the Admiralty? She feels certain that if she could get inside, a name would occur to her, a face would appear.

"What is your business here?" he asks.

She cannot answer his question. What is her business? A chill surrounds them, the air wet and cold.

"I'm sorry," she says and leaves the man, aware that a dozen pairs of eyes are upon her. Even the crippled know not to approach the guard.

Fog from the river rolls in as men wearing greatcoats emerge from the building and put their collars up. The light dims, an oily film settling over Stella's eyes. The wounded leave with their takings—enough to live on for another day? Gates open to let the motorcars out while some men walk. "Sister," someone calls to her.

His head is shrouded in a woolen scarf; perhaps the man comes out only in the fog. She can see one eye, a lipless mouth, two small orifices for a nose. Reaching into her pocket, she studies the coins in her palm and tucks several of them into the hand of the faceless man. Always look a patient in the eye.

When the man slips away, Stella strains to see if the uniformed officers are still walking or getting into their motorcars. But either they have gone or they are now swallowed up by the mist.

Reluctantly, Stella turns from the Admiralty into a brown opaque fog. Even in France, the mist was not this bad. She can hear a horse in the street but cannot see it. She takes out the map the newsboy drew; she will have to follow it in reverse. The question is no longer whether she will return to the Bridges in Bryanston Square, but whether she can find them.

On a bright November afternoon, several days after Stella's visit to the Admiralty, she follows Streeter up the stairs to the top of the house, a glass dome the size of a large room. Stella watches as a shaft of light travels along the rooftops of London, receding as if it were bowing.

"Good afternoon," Dr. Bridge says. He stands just in front of a faded yellow divan that describes a semicircle along the round room. "When my mother was alive," he says, gesturing to the potted fruit trees that make up the other semicircle, "these produced a bounty of blossoms and some fruit—a basket of oranges, if we were lucky. Now the trees remain dormant most of the year, though we do get a bit of foliage from time to time. We have always called this the orangery."

For a moment, Stella feels as though she has reached the roof of heaven. She is not sure she has ever been this high.

"The orangery was built in the last century and can't be seen from the street below us. Only a chimney sweep could spy on us. It's a magical place," Dr. Bridge says. "I've been much in love with it since I was a child."

He runs his hand along the bark of a tree. "My mother had a gardener whose sole task it was to tend to the trees. Personally, I preferred the blossoms to the oranges; the scent would linger in the stairwell. Many was the Sunday I sat in this dome finishing my schoolwork or reading—or, more likely, gazing out at the rooftops through the trees and trying to imagine a future."

"I like thinking of you as a boy," Stella says, aware that she is incapable of thinking of herself as a girl.

Dr. Bridge sits at one end of the divan and gestures for Stella to take a seat at the other end, so that they can face each other. "Thank you for seeing me today." Stella has agreed to the proposal Lily and Dr. Bridge made the day after Stella returned from the Admiralty. Stella would stay with the Bridges for a time while Dr. Bridge tried to diagnose and help her. Stella would work at the settlement house with Lily, and in return Stella would allow Lily to accompany her in the motorcar on her visits to the Admiralty so that she would not compromise her recovery from pneumonia.

She smoothes the skirt of her navy dress. Dr. Bridge has on a suit appropriate to his profession, though she wonders how it can be possible to have a spotless white shirt after having completed a surgery. In France, Stella never saw doctors in suits. They wore either uniforms or white aprons, which were never clean.

"How are you feeling?" Dr. Bridge asks.

"Better. I feel stronger each day. Why do you want to help me?"

The doctor frowns slightly. "During our first lunch together, I learned that you have debilitating pains in your legs, that you sometimes go deaf, and that you have lost your memory. At first I thought your symptoms merely physical, but I have begun to wonder if they don't in some way represent an injury in your mind. In the time since, I have made several inquiries among psychologists and psychiatrists as to your symptoms, and I have received the same reply each time. The common thought is that you are suffering from hysteria, but no psychologist or psychiatrist in London can take on female patients at this time. All are treating men who have returned from the front, or else they are serving on military medical boards. I am very sorry to have to tell you this."

Again, Stella is assailed by a powerful feeling that the solution to her problem lies at the Admiralty.

Dr. Bridge puts his hands together. "I may be able to aid you in recovering your memory."

"How?"

"As one colleague explained it to me, talk therapy has been effective in curing patients of their short-term ailments. We discussed the practice for some time, and he felt you and I might try it."

"And how would that be?"

"You talk, I listen."

Stella cannot help but laugh. "It seems awfully self-conscious."

"Well, yes," Dr. Bridge says. "But that's a hurdle we shall have to get beyond."

A sharp glint of sun lights up Dr. Bridge's spectacles, and he squints. He moves his head away. "I do believe that talking about what has happened to you may have some benefit. Sometimes it's necessary to speak of the worst in order to be cured."

"I wish I could go to your clinic and have my brain repaired."

"I don't think that can be what you want."

"Your job must be terrible at times," she says.

He shrugs. "It's my work. I find tremendous satisfaction in making an injured man well. Usually, I do it with a scalpel."

"I feel as though you are sharpening your scalpel for me."

"Do you?" he asks.

"You want to make me well."

"But with words, Miss Bain."

"Please call me Stella."

"Thank you. I'd invite you to call me August, but given the circumstances, I should remain as Dr. Bridge."

Stella ponders this. "Well, then, Dr. Bridge, I have something that I must tell you. This is difficult."

"I imagine every bit of this is hard for you."

"I'm convinced I did something unforgivable in my past life."

Dr. Bridge tilts his head. "Why do you say that?"

"I feel it."

"I see."

"It's a powerful feeling."

"You have guilt?"

"Yes, and something else. There's a kind of horror attached. Well, it's both more and less than horror—a sick feeling, a feeling of revulsion."

"Close your eyes now and try to relax. Does any sort of association with that feeling come to mind?"

Stella does as she has been asked. But inside her, there is only a black void.

"You lost your memory in early March," Dr. Bridge states. "You say you were injured. You'd been under bombardment?"

"Yes, several times."

"Your mind seems quite nimble and sharp. Your head was examined at Marne?"

"I'm told it was. I'm surprised you didn't send me to a hospital," Stella says.

"Would you have gone?"

She shakes her head. "I'm not a shirker. If it weren't for my desire to visit the Admiralty, I'd still be in France."

"I believe you."

"You're fascinated by my case, aren't you?" she asks.

"Yes, I suppose I am," Dr. Bridge says, crossing his legs. "From a professional point of view, it's deeply intriguing to treat a woman who has been under bombardment, but my goal is to make you healthier, as is the goal of any physician."

"Dr. Bridge, I want to know who I am. What if Stella Bain really is my name?"

He gazes at her as if contemplating whether to speak. "I have reservations. After your arrival here, my wife and I made inquiries at the War Office and the Red Cross as to a Stella Bain, VAD. I've been in touch with the American embassy, too. We've received no positive reply."

"I'm sometimes confused," she confesses. "When I first told you and Lily my name, I had a fleeting thought that Stella Bain might not be accurate."

"I plan to contact the field hospital in Marne. It may be more difficult, French bureaucracy being what it is. There may be no record of your joining that field hospital because you weren't there officially or because, for reasons unknown, no attempt was made to discover where you actually belonged. I imagine as soon as they found out you drove an ambulance, they might not have wanted to send you away. Do you intend to keep going to the Admiralty?"

That afternoon, Lily had accompanied Stella to the Admiralty in the green-and-tan Austin Mary Dodsworth drove. Lily had explained that she was happy to wait for Stella across the street for as long as Stella liked. But Stella asked Lily to leave her at the gate and then park some distance away, as she did not want to be observed in her frustrating quest. Stella had no better luck at the Admiralty than she had during her first visit.

"Yes, I do," Stella says.

Over the next several days, the Bridges and Stella settle into a routine. When Stella is not sketching, she often travels to the settlement house with Lily. There, she draws for children. In the afternoons, she tries to make it to the Admiralty, even though each visit seems a mere repetition of the first. Occasionally, Stella takes her meals with Lily and Dr. Bridge, but more often, she has a tray in her room. When Stella and Lily speak, the sessions in the orangery are never mentioned.

At their next meeting, a week later, Stella announces to Dr. Bridge that she has been drawing. "I purchased paper and a pencil on the afternoon after I left your house. I meant to write a note to you and Lily, but when I returned here, I began to draw instead. I used to sketch in France."

"I wondered what was in that packet," he says.

Unwanted heat rises to her face. "I was up hours last night."

Dr. Bridge opens his mouth to speak, but Stella cuts him off.

"I know, I know, I need rest. But I did sleep late this morning."

"May I see what you have?"

"The drawings are...I'm not sure how to phrase it...somewhat sinister, and this bothers me. I thought maybe you could help me with them."

Stella walks the packet over to Dr. Bridge and then returns to her spot on the divan. She glances everywhere but at him.

"I'm speechless," he says after he has studied the three drawings. "Do you have any idea, any idea at all, how good these are? They amaze me. You must—*you must*—have been an artist in your previous life."

Stella flushes with pleasure at his response, but then shakes her head to indicate that she is as perplexed as he.

"May we discuss these?" he asks.

"Yes."

"May I move closer to you?"

"Yes, of course."

Dr. Bridge sits next to Stella and sets the drawings on his knees. She is aware of his scent: a mixture of laundry starch and his own not unpleasant body odor. His proximity makes her nervous.

He studies the first drawing. It is of a room, a beautiful room, though not in the best condition. The plaster is chipped in places, and the sink is old. There are floral studies on the walls between the many windows. A plate of pears rests on a table.

"What does this room mean to you?" he asks.

"I feel it's a room I've been in. I'm aware of the room as an oasis. For a time, I'm happy there."

"What do you do in this room?"

"Do? I don't really know. Read? Sew? Draw? Polish the windows?"

"Simple pursuits."

"Yes."

"Is anyone in the room with you?"

"No," she answers. "The point is that I'm alone. I'm honest there. I can think. I feel replenished. The room is my secret and my haven."

"Outside the room," Dr. Bridge says, "you have drawn a kind of forest, which, as you suggested, seems rather menacing, or sinister, as you put it. I have never seen such trees, though they do remind me of misshapen trunks at the edge of a cliff or on a moor—no line is straight."

"Whatever is outside the house is evil."

"You set out to draw this particular room? Were you remembering something?"

"No, not a memory. It just came."

"What's the menace, precisely?" he asks in a gentle tone. She notes that her hands are shaking, and she has the distinct sense that the doctor would cover them if he could.

"I have no idea."

"You said you felt honest in that room, and you could think."

"Yes," she says, drawing a breath.

"Can you explain what you mean?"

"It's a sense that I can tell the truth in that room."

"To whom?"

She presses her lips together, thinking. "To myself, I suppose. There's no one else there."

"Do you think the room represents the interior of your mind?" he asks. "A place meant to be an oasis, a secret place where you once thought you could not be violated?"

"Or might it represent the way the war has violated me and all of us?" she counters. "That would explain the menace outside the room."

"Yes, that's possible."

But Stella can see that Dr. Bridge is not convinced.

"This is of a house, too," he says of the second drawing. "Is it the same as in the first? The woods behind it are similar."

"It's not the same house."

"A man is lying on a blanket. There's a picnic basket. Lovely food. Peaches and figs, it looks like."

Stella nods.

"The man has a telescope near him."

"Yes."

"Are you in this scene as well?" Dr. Bridge asks.

"I don't know. But the drawing makes me happy. I feel safer there than I did in the first. Possibly because of the man."

"You don't remember this man?"

"No. He might simply be a figment of my imagination."

"I'm fascinated by the telescope," the doctor says.

"I can't explain that."

"But still you have the menacing trees."

"I have a sense that he is not supposed to be there. Or maybe I'm not supposed to be there."

"And that's it? Does the drawing suggest anything else?"

Stella closes her eyes once again. She shakes her head.

Dr. Bridge tucks that drawing behind the others. When Stella sees the next drawing, she reaches over and puts both hands on top of it. "I didn't mean—" she says.

Dr. Bridge stares at her face. "You didn't mean to show it to me?"

"I didn't mean to draw it. I didn't intend for anyone to see it."

She begins to crumple the drawing, but he stops her hands. "Please, may I?"

She allows him to take the sketch from her.

A man on a bed, rumpled sheets covering his face. He is half undressed, and there seems to have been a struggle. A lamp is knocked over, and a mirror is broken.

"This makes me sick to look at," Stella confesses.

"Is the man dead?"

"I don't know."

Dr. Bridge shifts his position so that he can see Stella's face. "This can't be the same man as in the previous drawing."

"No."

"Is this man at the heart of your guilt and dread?"

"I don't know," she says. She has no idea what caused her to make this drawing. "It's terrible, isn't it?"

Dr. Bridge lays a hand on her shoulder. Gradually, she begins to feel calmer. "It's only a drawing, Miss Bain. Stella. It can't hurt you."

"But it does."

"Then we will leave this. We'll have to look at these drawings again, but I think not now."

At their next meeting, in late November, Dr. Bridge begins by talking of her sketches. "Your drawings may be your best links to the past. The difficulty with them is that they can resemble a thing that happened in real life, or they can be an invention of the mind."

"How will I ever know?" Stella asks.

"Well, you may not, and perhaps I won't, either. It's not simply the drawings themselves but the way they make you feel that might give us clues. The brain reacts in mysterious ways. As a cranial surgeon, I have had patients come through surgery entirely normal, yet on closer inspection I find that a man cannot identify individual letters on a page. Or that another is unreasonably angry, presenting a very different personality from the one he had before surgery. Or that yet another cannot actually speak his own name, though he can write it. These patients would seem to be fine otherwise."

A squall of rain sweeps across the glass dome, and Stella glances up. Nervously, she tucks her handkerchief farther into the cuff of her tea-colored dress. If she were not concerned about her money running out, she would buy material and sew another dress for herself.

"Is there any possibility that either of the two men in the drawings is the person you seek at the Admiralty?"

Stella's forehead is dotted with perspiration. "I don't know. My search for someone at the Admiralty feels entirely urgent. It's something I *must* do, not something I necessarily *wish* to do. It's complicated, isn't it?"

"Yes."

She rises and glides to the top of the stairs and stretches her arms behind her. For a bizarre moment, she thinks she might throw herself down the steps. She takes hold of the newel post and turns.

"So far you've been asking questions," she says. "And I've been trying to answer them."

"Yes, that's true. But as we progress, I hope that it will be you who will be doing most of the talking. The purest form of analysis, according to Sigmund Freud, is one in which the physician speaks not at all. You're familiar with Dr. Freud?"

"No."

"He is an Austrian neurologist who has developed a new theory of psychological treatment. But I believe Freud is talking about deep-seated neuroses and a period of many months, if not years, of therapy. We don't have that kind of time. You have a much more pressing concern if you are to live your life as a fully conscious being."

"I can't imagine what kind of life that would be," she says. "I feel as though I'm floating in a world in which I have no part. It's an extraordinary sensation, as if this were merely a dream, and at any moment I might wake up." She pauses. "What does Lily think of this? Of what we are doing? Of my continued presence in your house?"

Dr. Bridge leans back. "Do you mind if I smoke?"

"No, of course not."

He removes a square silver cigarette case from inside his

pocket, a case that clicks open at a touch. A matching lighter appears. Dr. Bridge selects a cigarette and lights it, then breathes in deeply. In France, the surgeons could do this one-handed.

"Lily has deep reservoirs of generosity and kindness," he says. "I believe she sees you as someone who needs help. She knows, however, that it is my assistance you need at this moment. As for our private conversations—yours and mine—I believe that's why she chose the orangery. We can't shut the door, for there isn't one, and yet no one, unless he or she happens to be sitting on the stairs right below us, can hear us. We're in the open, but not. This was her idea, and I readily agreed."

"While I was convalescing, Lily took my uniform dress to a seamstress to be used as a template for two new dresses for me. I thought that was very kind."

Dr. Bridge laughs. "I think it was more of a necessity than a kindness."

Overhead, Stella notes, the squall has ended. "Do you think, Dr. Bridge, that you and I might take a walk in the garden?"

He seems a bit discomfited. "That would be unorthodox."

"This entire quest is unorthodox."

"All right, then. Yes. I'll let Lily know, and I'll meet you in the front hall."

The garden, with its canopy of wet light in the trees, strikes Stella as splendid. She wonders if Dr. Bridge is as distracted by the glistening beauty as she is. She knows so little of the man, and yet she is beginning to form a picture: dedicated, cautious, loving toward his wife, and not without a little humor. After he closes the gate, they are showered with droplets from leaves that shake overhead. "Oh, this is lovely," she says, and then turns her face to Dr. Bridge. "Are you happily married?"

The doctor appears to find the question abrupt and surprising. "I am, yes. Quite happy. But . . ."

"It's rude of me to ask? Inappropriate?"

"No and yes," he says. "My personal life should remain outside our discussions, but this is somewhat complicated because you first came to my household and not to me as a doctor. So I think I can answer your question."

The umbrella he carries serves as a kind of walking stick. She watches as he rhythmically taps it along the path. He has a longer stride than she does, and silently they compromise to reach an even step.

"I fell in love with Lily at a cricket match," he begins. "I was a spectator, the guest of another party, but I couldn't help but notice a striking young woman who appeared to be enthralled by the match, sometimes frowning, sometimes laughing to herself. I guessed that she had a husband or a fiancé among the players in order to have such an assiduous interest. None of the other women seemed to be paying the slightest attention to what was happening on the pitch. Even I couldn't, having other matters on my mind. At the time, I had just started my clinic."

"When was this?"

"In 1908."

Stella cannot remember 1908. Or any year but the current one.

"When the match was over, I expected the young woman to greet one of the players, but she didn't. She joined two people who appeared to be her mother and sister, and after a time, a man, a player in uniform, came and sat with them, but he paid no special attention to Lily. I later learned that he was her brother, Tom, and that Lily enjoyed games of sport and their rules. She had been athletic in her school days and had won many ribbons and prizes, but of course there was no outlet for such activities after she left school. I think she misses extreme exercise, and had I not persuaded her to marry me, she might have become superb at tennis."

"You married her because she knew the rules of cricket?" Stella says teasingly.

Dr. Bridge laughs. "I married Lily for her beauty, her wit, and her compassion."

"Why will a man never say what is foremost in his mind when choosing a bride?"

"And what is that?"

"His physical passion."

"Well, I see that the frank VAD has returned," he says in an equally teasing tone. "You've spent too much time among the French doctors. When men say they marry for beauty, a healthy passion, as you say, is implied. But we should not be talking about me so much. Though I'm a bit of a novice at the talking cure, this much I'm sure of."

They enter a rose crescent, the canes dormant. Stella bends to a dead bloom as if to inhale the scent. She breathes deeply. Another garden of roses comes to mind. She pops her head up and turns to the doctor.

"I had a garden!" she exclaims. "Yes, I'm sure of it. I know how to deadhead roses and how to prune them."

"Where was this garden?"

Stella shakes her head. "I don't know."

"What was in the garden? Think hard."

Stella shuts her eyes. "Roses," she says. "Daylilies, yellow. Hydrangeas, poppies, and . . . and something by a fence that bloomed only once . . . what's the name? Big, blowsy flowers, white tending toward pink? *Peonies!*" She opens her eyes, thrilled to have this memory.

Dr. Bridge seems intrigued. "Go on," he says. "Describe the garden to me."

"There's a white fence." She pauses. "It extends from the corner of a house."

"One of the houses you drew?"

"No. Another house, but I can't see it. The garden is a rectangle, and there are blue flowers against one side of it. I don't know what they are."

"Who is with you in the garden?"

"No one," she says. "Well, maybe someone else is there, below eye level—a gardener, perhaps, but I can't see who it is. But . . . oh . . . it's going. The garden is going . . . ." She reaches out a hand as if she could pull it back. She looks up at Dr. Bridge. "How did that happen? Where has it gone?"

"It may return," he says.

"Oh," she cries out again, wrapping an arm around her waist. "It was so close. I could touch it. I could smell it."

"Let's sit here a minute," he suggests, guiding her to a nearby bench. "Can you see it at all?"

She gazes into an abyss. She feels bereft. "I know it only in my head as a recent memory in the same way I remember what I had for dinner last night. The immediacy is gone."

"Does it feel as if you had imagined it?"

"Not when it happened, but now I'm not so sure."

Dr. Bridge uses the tip of his umbrella to poke the dirt. "When one has a recollection from childhood," he explains, "the first few seconds are very real, but then it quickly becomes simply a memory. And this is a good thing," he adds, "or we should be paralyzed with too many seemingly real moments at once."

Stella sighs. "Yes, I suppose so."

"When you and I first walked in the garden, a nanny and three children entered. You were remarkably calm."

"Was I?"

"What struck me most was your aura of complete serenity. It was in your face, in the relaxation of your body."

She thinks a long moment.

"Try and see the nanny and children now," he directs.

Again, she shuts her eyes to do so. After a while, she begins to shake her head. "I can see them as a memory, but I can't re-create the feelings I had then."

Dr. Bridge stands and waits for her to join him. When they resume their walk, Stella glances back at the roses, hoping her garden will come alive again. She is reluctant to leave the area.

"The last drawing you showed me," he says. "Did that man in the bed hurt you?"

"I don't know."

"But the drawing made you extremely uncomfortable."

"Yes," she admits.

"Did you hurt him?"

"What an extraordinary question."

"Yes, it is. But you mentioned earlier that you felt a great guilt, that maybe you had done something terribly wrong. I wondered if the drawing came to you because it was a clue to that experience."

Stella has a sudden and intense desire to flee, but she cannot run away from the man beside her. Instead, she freezes rigid on the spot, unable to move a limb, unable to make sense of anything happening around her. She reaches for the back of her neck, certain that someone or something is about to grab her.

After a time, and she cannot say how long, her limbs loosen and she begins to wobble. A man holds her arm.

"Stella?"

Slowly, she turns her head. She recognizes the man beside her; his name is Dr. Bridge. But she cannot remember how it is that she knows him.

"What happened to you?" he asks.

She shakes her head. She does not understand. "I was afraid," she says.

"Of whom? Of what?"

"Something was behind me, and I knew that I had to get away. But I understood I couldn't get away. It felt as if I were frozen."

"I think you had a kind of seizure," the doctor says quietly. "There was no one behind you."

"How long did it last?"

"Almost ninety seconds by my watch."

"Ninety seconds!" Stella cries. Ninety incomprehensible seconds. "You have to help me," she pleads, turning to face him. "You have to help me fix this."

"I'll try. But right now I think we should get you home."

"Home," she repeats. "I have no home."

"You have one temporarily," he says.

"Am I getting worse?" she asks.

"I don't know," he answers.

A man wrestles with Stella, a man of ferocious strength. He pins her arms up beside her face on the pillow. She pushes as hard as she can with her legs, throwing off her blanket. She kicks the man in the stomach, and he makes a sound of pain. He is going to hurt her, she knows it. She tries to scream.

"Stella!" a man says in a firm voice. "Stella!"

She opens her eyes. Illuminated by the crack of light coming through the open bedroom door are the stern features of a man she knows, and for a second, she is not sure if he means to harm her or not.

"Stella," he says again.

Dr. Bridge gradually lessens the pressure on her wrists, as if testing whether or not she will strike out.

"What are you doing here?" she asks, breathing fast.

He lets go of her wrists and steps away from the bed. A wildness moves through her. She reaches down for her covers.

"A cry woke me," he explains, and she notices that he is in his dressing gown, colorless in the dim light. "At first I couldn't tell whether it was inside the house, but when I heard it again, I knew it was coming from upstairs. You were thrashing about and making frightened sounds." He gazes at her. "Awful sounds, as if you were being attacked. I was afraid you would hurt yourself, so I tried to wake you up."

Her body is shaking.

Dr. Bridge's hair is mussed and has drawn itself into a peak.

"Thank you," she says.

"Do you recall your dream? It must have been a nightmare."

"All I can remember is that a man was going to hurt me."

"You thought I was he when I tried to wake you."

Stella remembers the kick in the stomach. "I kicked you, didn't I?"

"Let's just say you gave it your all," he says and smiles. "I'll find Iris to bring you hot tea and clean sheets."

Stella does not protest.

"This man," Dr. Bridge asks. "Did you think he was going to kill you?"

Once again, she tries to recall. "I'm not sure. The man was on top of me. He meant to overpower me."

"I'm sorry you had to experience that," he says as Lily appears at his side. Lily moves toward the bed. She pours a glass of water from the pitcher at Stella's bedside.

"She had a nightmare," Dr. Bridge explains to his wife. "She was screaming."

"Oh, my poor dear," Lily murmurs as Stella takes a sip. Lily replaces the glass. "Here, let me just feel your forehead. No fever. Would you like me to return after you've changed and sit just outside the door while you sleep?"

"I'm really fine now," she says. "You should both go back to bed." In the light from the hallway, she can just make out Dr. Bridge's sleepy features.

Good morning," Dr. Bridge chirps as he reaches the top of the stairs a week after the incident in the night. It is mid-December, two weeks before Christmas. "You seem happy."

"Not as happy as you must be," Stella says, teasing him.

"Ah, then Lily told you," he says, taking a seat on the yellow divan.

"I asked. Otherwise I should have had to alert you to Lily's illness."

"Is she sick in the mornings?"

"She is. I'm sorry. I thought you knew."

"I'm up and out the door at least an hour before she wakes," he says. "Iris and Streeter must know as well."

"And Mrs. Ryan."

"Yes."

"They see the full, untouched breakfast trays. Lily must not have wanted to alarm you."

"Is it very bad?"

"She says it is when she first wakes, but after that she's fine, apart from a dull headache around five o'clock in the afternoon. Perhaps she is resting even now."

"Poor thing," he says.

"It's a joyous thing," Stella reminds him.

"Yes. Of course it is."

"I have new drawings."

"Have you?" he asks. "May I sit next to you?"

"Yes."

Stella slips the drawings from a paper packet. The first depicts a corner of the garden and its fence abutting yet another corner, that of a clapboard house. She has gone up the clapboards as far as she can go, at which point the lines become less distinct. With its irises in full bloom, the corner of the garden has been drawn with a more definite hand.

"Does the fact that the garden is more detailed than the house mean that you remember the garden better than the house?" Dr. Bridge asks.

"Yes," she answers. "I tried to see upward or over to a window, but when I attempted that, I knew my hand was just making it up. This morning I thought of another addition to the garden, so I may in time be able to draw the house."

"If you could draw the house with a window," he suggests, "perhaps you would be able to see inside. You might see a face or a piece of furniture or a clock."

"Possibly."

"You're quite sure this isn't the house you describe as your oasis or the house beside which you laid a blanket?"

"Quite sure."

The doctor's presence, with his scent of laundry starch and soap, reminds Stella of the incident in the night. She does not know how else to refer to it. She was screaming. He came in to wake her. That was all.

"Might this be a house you've drawn before?" he asks.

"I can't see its exterior."

The second drawing is again of the garden, but portrayed from a different angle. To one side of the path, a bed of flowers has been trampled upon.

"In another's hand," Dr. Bridge says, "this drawing might have had a fetching prettiness to it. In your hand, however, there is beauty, certainly, but it seems to hover inches from its opposite. Even the irises this time appear to be deep wounds of the flesh."

Stella is silent.

"There's no sign of a gardener or the person you thought was below you working."

"No," she says. "I can feel activity when I think about the garden, but when I draw it, there's no one there. I look for him, but I can't see him."

"Why are these flowers trampled?"

"I don't know. Perhaps this is from memory, or it suggests that something bad happened there. I did have a fleeting thought of soldiers trampling over gardens and fields as they marched."

"When you look at your garden drawings, what are you thinking?"

"My thoughts are complex," she answers. "I take pleasure in the garden itself, in bringing it to life, in remembering *something,* but there's frustration as well, because there's so much more to know. At what point did I have this garden—as a child or as an adult? To whose house was it attached? I can't make the pencil answer these questions. And I suppose there's also a feeling of pride in having discovered an ability to do this."

"I should hope so."

At their next session, Stella presents Dr. Bridge with a drawing of a face. A young man, with only some of his features depicted, looks straight at the viewer. One eye is vividly represented, but little of the right eye or indeed the face below it shows. The side of a nose as well as a half lip and a half chin have been completed. "Is this someone you saw in France?" he asks.

"I don't know."

A handsome face, even with its injuries. A full head of hair has been mussed about, as in a wind. The jawline is strong, the half lip full. The good eye and cheekbone suggest strength and steadiness.

"There are parts of the face missing," Dr. Bridge says.

"Yes."

"Why?"

"I can't remember."

"Why this face?"

"It was quite clear to me in my mind. I've done another."

The same man in profile. Grime in the wrinkles of his neck. Most distinctive is the shape of the head, with its almost Egyptian curve at the back.

"How I would have liked to have drawings of heads like these before I performed operations on the men I've treated," the doctor says. "But what a waste of your talents that would have been."

Stella cannot think of any better use for them.

"The man you've drawn here: is this someone you seek at the Admiralty?"

Dr. Bridge moves slightly away, and Stella turns to him. "I can't picture at all the man or woman I seek at the Admiralty. It's not a memory or a dream, merely a strong urge to go there."

"I'm sorry you haven't had better luck. Do you intend to continue, knowing how unlikely it is you'll encounter this person?"

She can feel herself blushing. "I'm certain that if I could get inside the building, I would find what I'm looking for."

"I may be able to help you with that," Dr. Bridge offers. "I'll go with you. There's an old friend of mine there, an officer. I'm sure he'll leave our names with the guard. Perhaps after Christmas week? I might have done this sooner for you, but I was hoping that you would let the concept of the Admiralty go and try to solve your problems through our discussions. But when I saw how our walk in the garden caused such a stir, I reconsidered."

Stella is amazed.

"We shouldn't be too hopeful about the visit," Dr. Bridge warns.

Two days later, after several pleasantries, Dr. Bridge asks to see the drawings again. He stops at the face. "I'm wondering if you connect this man with the garden."

The comment surprises her. "No."

"In sequence, you went straight from the garden to the man. In the last picture in the series of the garden, the flowers are trampled, and you yourself suggested France. Is there a link between tangled flowers and the face?"

Stella closes her eyes. "There must be," she says. "But I can't see anything apart from the obvious. Soldiers often ruined flowers in France. The landscape has been devastated. Perhaps he is a soldier?"

"Or maybe something at that house, in that garden, was ruined, causing you to make the link between the garden and France."

"I have another drawing," she says, wanting to change the subject.

He takes the paper from her and sets it on top of the others. "I take it this is the OAB? The Admiralty?"

"The side entrance."

"You couldn't finish the man coming out the door."

Stella shakes her head.

"Is this the person you hope to meet?"

"Possibly."

"It's interesting he's not in uniform."

A uniform never occurred to Stella. The faceless man is tall and well dressed.

"You've written 'Unfinished' over the drawing," Dr. Bridge says.

"I was frustrated."

She has drawn the lines of masonry, the wrought-iron gate, and the figure of the guard who stands just outside the entrance. The frame of the drawing encompasses the doorway and the immediate environs. She has depicted the back end of a motorcar waiting at the right-hand side of the page. Stella has filled in the rest of the sketch with lines that show depth, shadow, and texture.

When the drawing was true, the pencil moved with ease. When she began to stray from authenticity, the marks had to be erased.

"It's as if the drawing were trying to tell you something," Dr. Bridge says, lightly tapping the sketch with the backs of his fingernails.

"Maybe," she says. "When the drawing was almost completed, I put the tip of my pencil to the paper and waited. I tried to erase all preconceptions. It was a man and not a woman I sought—I was sure of this. I made soft circles with my pencil, hoping the touch of lead on paper would open a door in my mind. But the frustration built again."

Stella has drawn trousers, one knee bent as it descends a step. The angle of the knee and of the body suggest haste. Of course, she thinks now. It is raining. The man has no overcoat or umbrella.

She has perfected the tailoring of his suit coat. His arms are full of folders, like those of a schoolboy hurrying home. The figure is not that of a boy, however, but of a man, slim but not emaciated.

"The neck and face of the man descending the steps seemed to vanish from the drawing as if—*poof!*—by magic," she explains. "But I've never seen that man in any doorway of any city."

"I wonder if that's true," Dr. Bridge ventures.


Just before Christmas and before the Bridges are to leave for Lily's family's place in Greenwich, they give Stella a present during dinner. Inside a beautifully wrapped box is an abundance of good sketching paper, a series of pencils of different sizes, several erasers, and—the highlight of the gift—a set of watercolors. Though she cannot remember ever having celebrated Christmas, Stella is touched by their generosity. "I shall try a watercolor of your lovely drawing room as my present to you," she offers.

"You have a wonderful talent," Lily states. "Simply allowing you the space and time to pursue it is gift enough for August and me. Don't you agree, August?"

"I do indeed."

Stella would like to know who actually purchased the supplies. Lily? Dr. Bridge? The two of them together?

Invited to accompany them to Greenwich, Stella decides instead to stay home on the grounds that she would feel uncomfortable among strangers at such an intimate family affair. Lily and Dr. Bridge protest, but in the end, they leave Stella on her own with Mrs. Ryan and Streeter, who presents Stella with a roast beef dinner on Christmas Day.

"Oh, but this is too much," she blurts before realizing how much work it was for Mrs. Ryan to make the meal, and that both she and Streeter have taken time away from their own holidays to be with her. "But I shall happily try," she says, looking up and smiling.

A heavy snow falls while the Bridges are gone. Because Stella doesn't remember ever having seen snow and is keen to go out into it, she asks Streeter if he has any rubber boots she might wear. He finds her a pair that are too big, but she is pleased to have them. During the storm, she makes her way to the gate of the garden in the middle of Bryanston Square. How silent it is! She forges a path to the rose crescent and marvels at the shapes the snow has made on the dead blooms. She would like to know where the garden she drew was located. She gazes again at the snow-blurred houses that surround the garden. The only indication they are inhabited is the smoke rising from the chimneys. She thinks of Dr. Bridge in Greenwich. What do families do on a holiday when they are all together? Is Dr. Bridge an entirely different man in such a situation?

After the Christmas holiday, Dr. Bridge and Stella once again find themselves in the orangery.

"Living with memory loss has meant a life of frustration,"

Stella says. "How did the soldiers I met in the hospital camp survive memory loss? Did they go mad, as I sometimes think I will?
Occasionally, in my room, I want to lash out and hit something
with all my strength. Again and again."

She puts her hand on a drawing similar to the last one he saw,
that of the man at the Admiralty. She looks up at Dr. Bridge. "I
believe I'm getting closer to recovering my memory—day by day,
even hour by hour. But in the interim, my frustration is growing.
It was easier, I think, when I simply accepted that my past was
gone. I was calmer then."

"But ill nevertheless."

"Yes."

"You feel better now?"

She turns away and stares at a barren orange tree. "That would
be hard to say."

"I have an idea," he says. "Can you draw a self-portrait?"

"Here? Now?"

"Yes. I think it might be a good idea. Have you tried it before?"

"No."

"Will you do it?"

She hesitates. "I'll have to fetch my pad and pencil."

"By all means," he says, gesturing toward the stairs.

When she returns, Stella sits near Dr. Bridge so that he can
see as she draws. She opens her pad and selects from three pencils
the one with the best point. "Streeter sharpens these for me," she
says.

"Does he?"

She draws a line and stops. "This is awkward," she says. "Embarrassing. I do this only in private. I feel as though I'm about to undress myself."

"Pretend I'm a patient you're trying to distract."

"Where are you wounded?" she asks.

"I've been shot in the leg. It's supposedly healing well, though I'm liable to whine with the pain. Also, I'm cranky."

She smiles. "Then I shall make you behave," she says and begins to move her pencil.

She draws herself inside a hospital camp. She sketches out her shape in uniform, her posture bent toward a wounded soldier. She leaves that to fill in the background: cots, soldiers, surgeons, nurses, canvas, and bandages. Men sleeping. Men receiving medicine. A man, clearly dead, his mouth open as if in a long yawn. There is a bucket for water; a glimpse into another tent, where surgery is being performed. She draws swiftly and with purpose, removing lines from time to time with her gum eraser. She applies shadow and light and gradations of what is meant to be color. She wants to convey the blue of the officers' uniforms, the red crosses on the nurses' bibs. She wishes to describe the texture of the canvas of the tent and to see through it a kind of daylight beyond.

"My God," Dr. Bridge says, startling her. "Any newspaper would employ you this very day. To be able to illustrate so well and with such detail! I feel as though I'm seeing something I've only been able to imagine. Really, Stella, this is remarkable."

When everything has been completed to her satisfaction, she fills in her uniform, the folds of the skirt, the texture of the fabric, her hands as they flow from the starched white cuffs, the roundness of the bib meant to hide the breasts, the folded cloth that becomes a cap.

She pauses.

"I can't do it," she says, her pencil stopped at a place that might be a chin.

"Are you sure?"

"I'm sure. I see it all, everything. Except for my face. The pencil just quits."

"You can see your face in a mirror?"

"Yes, but I can't draw it."

"Rest a moment," Dr. Bridge suggests. "Close your eyes. Try to see the face."

She lets the pencil drop into her lap, stretches her fingers, and then shakes her hand out. Only then does she ease her head back against the cushion. Above her, gray clouds spin about the dome. She closes her eyes. Her throat elongated, she feels vulnerable. She can hear Dr. Bridge breathing quietly beside her.

After some minutes, she sits up. "It's no good. It won't come. I have no face to draw."

"You have a beautiful face," he blurts out.

She believes he meant the compliment as encouragement. Instead, it sounded like an unintended slip. Can a man possibly care for a woman who is not herself? A woman who, with any luck, might change into someone else? Can a woman who is not herself truly care for another?

She gathers her materials and stands. "So you'll take me to the Admiralty?" she asks quietly. She hands him the unfinished drawing.

"We'll go a week from today."

The rain spits sideways in great gusts as Mary Dodsworth brings the motorcar around. Dr. Bridge's black umbrella, with which he hopes to shield Stella on the way from the house to the vehicle, blows inside out the moment he opens it. Dr. Bridge and Stella run for the car and duck inside, their outer garments beaded up with water. Dr. Bridge has made arrangements with a rear admiral he knows for a noon appointment at the Admiralty. Between them, it has been decided that Albion Tillman will keep Dr. Bridge and Stella waiting in an area through which most personnel pass either going to or coming from the canteen during the lunch hour. The delay will be tedious, but it is, after all, the point of the excursion: Stella will have an opportunity to scan the passersby for the man she seeks.

Stella has her uniform on, the white bib over the blue dress, her hair fixed neatly under the white cloth that ties in the back to make a cap.

"You remind me of the Miss Bain I met when you came to us. But now you have regained your health. Are you sure the uniform is wise? Someone may query you as to your posting."

"I'll be taken more seriously in my quest to find my 'brother,' who went to sea to participate in the Battle of Jutland and from whom I've heard nothing."

"Tillman knows this is a false request."

"Yes, but we may encounter an underling. I've found that, for a woman, a uniform enhances her status."

"For a man as well," Dr. Bridge says beside her, and she imagines he may be nursing that old wound. They journey along George Street, through Baker Street, to Oxford Street, none of them marked with a signpost.

Is it possible that in a matter of hours she will find the man she is looking for?

When Mary Dodsworth gives Dr. Bridge's name at the Admiralty gate, the Austin is allowed to pass through. Stella sucks in a long breath as they reach the courtyard. Already this is farther than she has ever been.

Despite an attempt to appear normal, she stumbles when Dr. Bridge helps her out of the vehicle.

"Steady now," he says in a quiet voice. "You're distressed at the mystery surrounding your brother's disappearance, but you're not afraid to be here. In fact, the opposite. You demand information."

"Yes, of course," she says, but something more complicated than fear grips her.

Inside the stately lobby, now defaced with handwritten signs and temporary desks, boots ring out with authority on the marble floor as men in uniform come and go. Dr. Bridge and Stella visit reception and inquire about an appointment with Rear Admiral Albion Tillman. The receptionist, a woman in a Wren uniform, makes the call and tells them that there will be a slight wait. Would they care to take one of the benches against the marble wall? She will alert them when Tillman becomes available.

Stella and Dr. Bridge settle themselves to wait at least an hour, as prearranged. She notices other civilians on benches, one or two of whom appear to be in severe distress. She makes a mental note to stop as she and Dr. Bridge pass by the front gate to hand a coin to a beggar.

She does not know what she is looking for, but hopes she will know it when she finds it. Conversation with Dr. Bridge is all but impossible, not only because she is riveted to each face passing by but also because even whispers can be heard in the echoing chamber. When she and Dr. Bridge are both staring at an individual, that person stares at them in return, which, she supposes, is all right, since the person may recognize Stella before she recognizes him.

When, after an hour, Dr. Bridge's name is called, he stands. Stella is now confronted with an inescapable fact: her time spent searching for a face is over. An escort comes forward to take them to Tillman's office. They follow the junior officer, Stella leading, Dr. Bridge behind.

Albion Tillman, an overweight man in his forties, a man who sports a curved gray mustache and many medals, stands when they enter. Dr. Bridge thanks him for seeing them.

"What's this all about, then?" the officer asks when they are seated and introductions made. "I don't think you mentioned that Miss Bain would be in uniform still." He turns to Stella. "Are you returning to France soon?"

"No, sir, I am not. I put it on because I thought that if we encountered anyone else here, I might be taken more seriously."

Though he is amiable enough with Dr. Bridge, Tillman has a stern visage. Stella worries that the high-ranking officer might say that her being in uniform is unethical. Perhaps there is even a regulation concerning the matter. She finds she is holding her breath.

"Yes, quite right," Tillman says. "Some of the men here see a civilian woman and assume she's one of the bereaved who've come to ask for our help. And you would be surprised at how much the men who have seen action dislike civilians."

"I am sorry to have come under false pretenses," Stella says.

"Have you had any luck?" Tillman asks, looking at both of them.

"I'm afraid not," Dr. Bridge answers as Stella lowers her head, embarrassed by her odd search and dismayed by the results.

"To lose one's memory must be as painful as losing a limb," Tillman says. "More, I should imagine. Are you sure that you will find the person you are looking for here?"

"It is not a certainty."

The room is smaller than Stella imagined. The combination of a high ceiling and the closeness of the walls makes her feel as though she were caught in a box, and a musty one at that. Or perhaps it is Tillman's bulk that causes the chamber to lose its scale. The smell of wet wool is pervasive.

"Any sight or sound that helps us is worth following up," Dr. Bridge comments.

"Yes, just so," agrees Tillman, who seems as puzzled as he was before Dr. Bridge's explanation. "I imagine you want to keep this particular meeting as brief as possible. I wish you luck, Miss Bain, in your difficult endeavor. We should all pray for a swift end to this terrible war." And with that, Tillman abruptly stands again, dismissing them both.

*     *     *

Stella's steps are slow as they leave the rear admiral's office with the escort, who has waited for them. The junior officer must think the meeting amazingly brief. Or perhaps such pro forma interviews are common. The escort leaves them at the reception desk.

"I think we should like to sit a minute," Dr. Bridge explains to the woman in the cubicle. "We have received difficult news today."

"Of course," the Wren says, glancing at Stella.

Noticing the heavier foot traffic inside the hall, Dr. Bridge guides Stella to a bench similar to the one they were on before. "I'll wait with you until you are ready to go."

"Thank you," she says.

"Are you all right?" he asks.

"Yes." She pauses. "No. Nothing is normal. How can it be? I don't yet know who I am. I may discover, when I know my identity, that I'm not a good person at all. I fear that I'm not. I seek my identity, and yet I'm afraid of it. But I'm more afraid of never knowing."

Stella speculates about how the two of them look to the hallway full of uniformed men and women: a civilian man, well dressed but perhaps betraying his eagerness to leave the building, and a woman in a pristine VAD uniform with her shoulders slumped and her eyes seeming to look more inward than outward.

"Actually, I'm ready to go now," she says, her voice barely more than a whisper.

"Are you sure?" Dr. Bridge asks.

"Yes, quite sure."

\*    \*    \*

The two repeat the exercise several times in the early weeks of
1917. On each occasion, Dr. Bridge telephones Albion Tillman
in advance to make the request. Sometimes, for their "meetings,"
they do not meet with Tillman at all, but rather sit with the junior officer in an anteroom. Once, a Wren makes them tea and
puts them in a waiting area. On each day that they go, Dr. Bridge
and Stella wait in the hall an hour at lunchtime and then spend a
few minutes back on a bench before they leave. Stella knows she
cannot ask Dr. Bridge to waste any more time at this charade. He
has been exceptionally generous, given that he does not believe
she will be successful here.

"This has been a fool's errand," Stella insists at the end of the
fifth visit. "It has been extremely kind of you to have arranged
these meetings. But I thought, when I realized how our request
must have appeared to that poor exhausted Wren, that I was ad-
dled in my thinking. Not only that, but being in uniform again
and being in this place has given me the idea that I should return
to France."

"Nonsense!" Dr. Bridge exclaims. Heads turn. In a lower voice,
he adds that they will talk about this when they get back to
Bryanston Square.

Stella stands. She turns her head away from the passing crowd,
the constant murmuring of voices. Yes, she must return to
France. What possible good is she doing here in London? Dr.
Bridge will disapprove. VADs are needed at home, too, he will
tell her—as someone once told him about doctors.

As they near the double doors, Dr. Bridge steps forward to
open one. Behind her, Stella can hear the smart rap of boots on
marble.

"Etna?"

Stella stops and gentles herself into a still posture. She considers the name.

"Etna Bliss?"

Stella half turns toward the voice. A ginger-haired officer has spoken to her. She sways slightly. Dr. Bridge guides her to a bench. She has a memory. She knows the man's name.

"Samuel."

As Dr. Bridge makes her sit, Stella feels each new memory as an electric shock.

The officer, in Canadian uniform, kneels directly in front of Stella.

"Etna," he says again. "Etna Bliss."

The name no longer a question.

She digs her fingernails into Dr. Bridge's wrist.

"What is it?" he asks, bewildered by the exchange.

"I have children," she says.

*Thrupp, New Hampshire, 1896–1915*

*An* abandoned house, once white with pride, left alone to age. A man sets a blanket on the grass. He is older than she, thirty to her twenty.

"My astrophysicist," she wants to say aloud, laughing at herself. What does she know of lunar distances, solar flares, orbiting planets, colliding bodies?

She sits, then lies, upon the blanket. He tilts his head, a sentry alert to toneless insects, noisy sparrows. Hard knots of thread press against the back of her cotton dress. His arm is rusty with fine red hairs.

He is engaged to another.

She is engaged to another.

In a different century, they would be stoned to death.

He kisses her face, his skin skimming the surface of hers. Her body floats upward into his.

He says he has never been so happy. When he tells her of his love, she says that hers is greater. They laugh, and delirium presses them together.

A partial undressing, a milky gleam upon a thigh, this mundane place unique. She cannot do again what she is doing for the first time.


She runs through the streets of town, mad with disbelief. She squanders everything she has of character to confront her lover. Houses laugh at her, or smirk.

Breathless, she arrives at the forbidding family facade from which she will soon be barred. She stands in the foyer and cannot believe in the mask *that has fallen over her lover's face. From a corner, a mother appears and watches.*

*"I go to Toronto tomorrow to be married," her lover says, his eyes and face unknown to her. She wants to beg, go down on her knees, but she catches sight of a brother, younger and impressionable, who gazes at her with wonder from another room.*

*When her lover shuts the family door behind her, she stands on the wooden steps. The houses are smug now, politely looking aside.*

*Years later, passion merely a faded photograph, she faces another man in another room, a stolid Dutchman she will never love. But pity blossoms and ensnares her and causes her to make a grave mistake. She has failed to count the nights of her future. She has never known the anguish of an unhappy marriage bed. She has not imagined that a house can become a fortress, a prison.*

*Her husband wants to possess her fully, but she holds something in reserve. Something indefinable, her own, that he can never touch.*

*She has children, beautiful babies. They make a playhouse of the prison. Together, they wait for squirrels beneath the trees; together they shake the bushes, hoping for birds. They plant a garden, the crooked rows soon blistered with colorful blooms. They walk through leaves and snow. They play innocent games of castles and battles, of magic and buried treasure. Their gentle footsteps do not disturb the earth.*

*She becomes a child with them at dusk, when bat loops make them dizzy. Her children hide with her in tree trunks. They fashion nests in her hair; she makes cakes with sticky frosting. She teaches them their lessons, then sends them off to school. She is happy in that house only when her children are safe within its walls.*

* * *

*A room, a cottage, the plaster chipped in places. Her own, with floral studies on the walls. She is honest in that room, and she can think. She has a sink, a plate of yellow pears. She reads, she sews, she draws. A woven rug covers a scrubbed floor. Her windows are precious jewels that she polishes.*

*Here she is replenished. The cottage is her secret and her haven. When it is taken away from her, she empties out to silence.*

*A party, Champagne bubbles, a flute that slips from her fingers. The younger brother from years ago, her lover's sibling in another room, now grown but unmistakable. Unwittingly, a rival for a post her academic husband believes is his. The man she married seethes, becomes a twisted creature with a selfish agenda. The younger brother—merely decent, merely kind—wins the post despite his desire to disappear. To her, he offers simple friendship, nothing more. He remembers her face as she stood in that family foyer so many years ago and tells her that it has always been the standard by which he has measured love.*

*Another bed, and she is frightened. A man has her body laid out upon his own, a piece of cloth on his pattern. She faces outward, staring at the ceiling. The man, her husband, covers her mouth with his hand, the air so hot and wet she has trouble breathing. He tramples over every memory of their marriage, and yet the curtains at the window do not move; the electric lamps still burn. Her husband plays her body with fat fingers. He touches every part of her he thinks he owns. She has children in another room, a letter on a table. She will not wake the children. She will not send the letter.*

*He tears the cotton of her blouse. Lust, that beautiful hunger, turns ugly in his hands. Love has never been in that house, and he is mad with rage—this violent act unique.*

*Her husband uses his innocent daughter to destroy the reputation of his rival, that younger brother from years ago, and causes him to risk his life in France. The trenches are awash with a mixture of flesh and muck. Great bursts of shrapnel tear bodies into pieces. The soldiers, with their guns and boots, destroy every living thing. A face is gone, a spine. The limbs pile up in buckets. The man her husband sent to France drives an ambulance, a pacifist at war. She tries to find him to make amends.*

*If she locates the man her husband sent to France, will he know her face, its features contorted by terror and by guilt?*

*Wherever she is billeted, she inquires about the man from America. Records are imperfect; they are often lost in shelling. He might be one mile from her or sixty. Sentries stand guard outside the tents, alert to guns and gas. She is covered with blood and worse each morning. Her mind is injured. Whose is not?*

*Camiers, November 1915*

On a gray day, the world seems of a piece: a mechanized earth-works that blows bodies into the air, tosses them into the mud, ferries them to the field hospitals, and then deposits them on stretchers in tents, to be cut open by steel scalpels. On sunny days, fleeting memories of past pleasures are pointedly out of sync. Today is such a day, the blue sky and the distant Channel frightening.

A surgeon replaces a portion of a man's skull with silver plate. Etna Bliss, nurse's aide, stands at attention, delivering instruments, taking the fouled ones from the nurse to be cleaned and boiled, stepping up when ordered to mop blood from a wound. Dr. Eliot, like many of his colleagues, works in silence, though all around them there is chaos.

Conversation is reduced to nouns—verbs and adjectives having been shelled away. "A thermometer, *if* you please." "From the front, sir, with blisters."

Etna has been at Camiers with the Royal Army Medical Corps for ten weeks, from early September, 1915, to this day, which, if they were in America, would be Thanksgiving. There will be no holiday on the French coast.

\* \* \*

That Etna has children in New Hampshire sounds a low, dark note in her womb, a sinking sensation similar to the ones she experienced while giving birth to Clara and to Nicky. That she has left them hits her anew each time, the truth rendering her momentarily paralyzed.

"You will not be granted custody," a fatuous lawyer warned her in New Hampshire in a tone of voice that suggested dark punishments if she tried to contest this. "Your husband is dean of the college and has deep financial resources. It was not he who wanted a divorce. It was not he who had a secret cottage."

The law supports a man who raped his wife and corrupted his child, but will not help a woman who wants only to be the mother of her children.

She will make her way back to her children regardless of the contract she has signed, of the distance that separates her from them, of the urgency of her work. How she will do this, she cannot yet imagine.

The ward nurse, a nun, orders Etna to remove a dressing that holds a soldier's entrails inside his body. When Etna protests that such an action will kill the man, who looks more like a boy, the sister becomes insistent. Because the soldier will die before the day is over, the sister wants the procedure done as soon as possible so that she can use the bed for a man worth saving. Etna is certain that such a request—to kill a man by means of medical intervention—is unethical, even if the man will die anyway. Where exactly did medical procedure break down? A man cannot survive a wound to the entrails. The young British soldier ought to have been left outside the medical tent and put in the area where the dying are made as comfortable as possible. Bad luck for this soldier, because now he must be treated.

When she is nearly finished, the soldier comes awake, unaware that half of him is in an enamel basin below the cot. He stares at her, and she smiles, knowing that hers is likely to be the last face he will ever see.

All this in a canvas tent full of abysmal smells and screams. The screams of the injured, yes, Etna expected those. But she was not prepared for the startled gusts from the unseasoned nurse's aides. Or from a doctor, yelling in frustration at a succession of deaths despite heroic efforts. Or from a ward sister, exhausted to the breaking point, demanding, in a shrill voice, that the stretcher bearer *move it.*

Phillip Asher, with his dual citizenship, is, according to her husband, who was taunting her at the time, an ambulance driver with the British Red Cross in France. He left the ruination of his life as he knew it in America.

Everywhere Etna goes, she asks for Phillip Asher. She queries nurses, ambulance drivers, orderlies, even the wounded.

When people ask her why this man, Phillip Asher, is so important, she answers simply that she owes him.

Etna makes a request for dismissal.

"Are you ill?" asks Captain Richardson of the RAMC.

"No."

"Are you suffering from hysteria?"

"No."

"What is it, then?"

"I have children."

"We all have children."

"Yes, but—"

"I don't see any mention of children here on your application."

"Well, no, I was—"

Richardson interrupts her even as he is reading the papers in front of him. "You wanted to appear to be single to get to France, and then when you got here, you changed your mind."

Etna remains silent. He will not understand her story.

"Back to your post at once, Nurse, and do not bother us with future requests. Morale is terribly important, you must know that."

"Yes, sir."


Next time, when asked if she suffers from hysteria, Etna will answer in the affirmative. She might even go to her superiors with her own diagnosis. It is hysteria, is it not? A perfectly reasonable response to her recent past? To her current surroundings?

If she were to insist on going home, who would stop her? She is technically under the auspices of the Royal Army Medical Corps, but really she is just an American volunteer. She will be regarded as a disappointment, but that hardly matters now. She may be required to pay back the cost of her passage, and she will somehow do that.

But if she does leave, where will she go, and how will she get back to New Hampshire? She can probably talk her way across the Channel, but what will happen once she disembarks? She knows no one in England except for the one man she cannot ask for help—Samuel Asher, her childhood lover, seconded to the Royal Navy from Toronto. She will have barely two pounds sterling in her pocket, and that only if she is paid for time served. She must find a job in England and work at it long enough to accrue the money for passage across the Atlantic. To do that might take many months. Would it not be better, then, to see her contract through and be sent back as promised when her year has ended? she asks herself as she cleans bedpans and holds the hands of the wounded.

She soaks bandages in ice-cold water and knows precisely how thick with red the water should be before removing the bloody mass of cotton. She rinses, and rinses again, until the bandages are pale pink, after which she will bleach them. There are no gloves for nurse's aides, only tongs. Her hands redden, as if by the blood itself. After the bleaching, the bandages will be boiled.

In December, the ward sister orders Etna to appear in the matron's office. Captain Richardson, who once refused her request to be dismissed, leans against the front of the matron's desk, his arms folded over his chest.

"Nurse Bliss," he says. "I like your age. Your maturity, I should say. You have demonstrated maturity on the wards."

"Thank you."

"We won't discuss your bizarre request for dismissal."

"No."

"Requisitions needs an ambulance driver immediately. You wrote on your application that you can 'drive a large car.' Is that true?"

"Yes, sir."

"It would be a truck with a rough transmission."

Etna nods, never having dealt with a rough transmission. The Cadillac Landaulet required only the push of a button to start.

"Three of our drivers were killed when a convoy was shelled last night."

"I am very sorry to hear that," she says, deciding instantly not to imagine the shelling.

"Matron has been kind enough to let us borrow you from time to time," the officer explains, and Etna guesses that Matron cannot have done this happily.

The RAMC gives her a kit of a heavy woolen skirt, a woolen shirt, a fur-lined jacket, a pair of gloves, a belt, goggles, binoculars, a gas mask, a canteen, and a sturdy hat with a brim, around which she ties a long white scarf made from a bedsheet.

The wood-paneled truck has red crosses on each side and on the roof. Inside, three stretchers hold the wounded. The bus can accommodate seven men if they are sitting.

Etna no longer has room in her head for contemplation. Her world consists of stretchers and dressings, of long splints, short splints, legs, and arms. Her universe smells of iodine, of sweaty surgeons in dirty white coats, of the engine exhaust used to heat the ambulances. She sees herself from a new angle when she sees herself at all: two-thirds nurse's aide, one-third ambulance driver, used at will by the powers that be. She finds tremendous relief in doing and not knowing.

The scheduled three-month leaves are canceled due to heavy shelling. No word is given as to when they might be rescheduled.

She imagines the world she came from as stopped in time, pre-served, one that will start up again when she returns. She clings to this construct as the wounded do to hope.

At ten o'clock on a February morning in 1916, the sleet outside her tent pinging off the metal poles, Etna starts to remove her heavy jacket so that she can sleep her allotted hours. The attack began at dawn. Etna and a man named Wilson were ordered to be in place at the Regimental Aid Post before the shelling began. She knows she will never be able to talk about the war when it ends—especially the way the officers send men into battle with preparations already in place for their death and wounding, a ma-chine anticipating a high percentage of breakdowns.

A benefit of Etna's dual responsibilities is that she now has her own bell tent. Because of her irregular schedule, it will not do to be awakened during her four or six hours of sleep or to wake an-other who might be exhausted.

A nurse's aide pokes her head between the flaps. "You're wanted outside," she says.

"By whom?" Etna asks, about to explain that she has just fin-ished her shift.

"A man."

"A man?"

"He says he knows you."

"Did he give his name?"

"I understand you've been looking for me," Phillip Asher says when Etna emerges from the canvas.

Etna doubles over as if from a blow. She always thought it

would be she who found him, not the other way around. His presence seems too tangible, even though she has been hoping for it for months. She feels a hand on her arm, helping her upright. When she sees his face, she covers her mouth.

"Are you all right?" Phillip asks.

"I came here to find you," she blurts out as a greeting.

She examines her friend—the water dripping off his cap, the lively gray eyes, the dark blond mustache, the half smile on his face—pleased that he has surprised her, even more tickled, she thinks, by her masculine uniform.

"Phillip," she manages, believing and not believing. "What are you doing here?"

"What are *you* doing here is the better question."

"I drive an ambulance. I'm a nurse's aide." She tries to tuck her hair back up into the knot that has come partially undone.

"At the same time?"

"More or less, wherever I am needed."

"It's filthy weather."

"Let's stand in here."

Something inside her flickering to life, Etna leads Phillip into the marquee where operations are performed. "I've been searching for you," she repeats.

"Why?"

She cannot give him, here and at this hour, her apology. He is soaked through and shivering. On the other hand, she worries that he might go off and not return. "I came to find you to make amends for what my family did to you," she says and thinks, no, that is wrong. "For what *my husband* did to you. I also hoped to persuade you to return to America. My daughter would then have a chance to recant her false testimony that you...that you...touched her. She could save your good name, and you could forgive her."

"There's no need," Phillip says, bewildered.

"Yes, there is. What happened to you at his hands was..." She searches for the right word. "Vile."

They both smell of wet wool and petrol. "I never forgave your daughter because there was nothing to forgive. It was clear she was manipulated. I hope you will one day tell her that. I am not returning to America."

"Will you think about it?"

He smiles to appease her. "I'm stationed at Étaples," Phillip says. "Just down the coast. I had to see if what one of the other drivers said was true—that you were asking for me. When I got to the Regimental Aid Post, an orderly said a woman was looking for me."

"How wonderful." She, too, is shivering inside her wool jacket, but not from the cold. "You're all right? You're not hurt?"

"Not a scratch."

In the brief silence between them, she can hear men gasping, choking. "Gassed," she says.

"I know the symptoms."

"Those are the worst cases. It's horrible."

He examines her with curiosity. "There's a village not far from here, maybe two and a half miles, with a café. Do you have any time now? I have a few hours before I have to get the truck back."

She thinks of her allotted six hours of sleep before her nursing shift begins. "I'll just have to change my clothes. Go back up the road and park at the stone barn. I'll be there as soon as I can."

*   *   *

Etna puts on a civilian dress she has hidden in her trunk—a plain gray wool. She peers into a small mirror on a table. She can make out her face and hair but cannot take in the whole of her dress. She slips her regulation cloak over it.

Having her own tent is ideal for an escape. Walking out with a man, even if he were her brother, is cause for serious reprimand and possible punishment. There are a hundred ways in which the head sister can make a misery of a VAD's life. Etna enters into the thick, dark woods along a well-worn path and emerges onto a dirt road not far from the stone barn. Phillip drives an ambulance that, unlike hers, has been painted white, a target if ever she saw one—though the men she works with believe the opposite: at least the red cross indicates a vehicle that should not be bombed, they argue. She runs the rest of the way, opens the passenger door, and climbs up. He puts the truck in gear.

"You really drive an ambulance?" he asks as they bump along the road toward the village.

"I do," she says, smiling. She loves the sensation of fleeing, of escaping. She has always loved it.

"You used to drive a car in Thrupp," he says.

"I did."

"I remember your wild hats and the scarves trailing behind."

"I remember you in the cottage, your hand raised up high under the chandelier, as if you were about to dance," she adds, and immediately wishes she had not. She has strayed too close to the heart of the matter, as if she had said a line too soon in a play. Clara was often in the cottage when Phillip visited.

"How can you see?" she asks after a time, watching the ice build up on the windshield.

"I can't. I'm just hoping there's no one out walking."

"I wouldn't think so in this," she says as she sits up tall to see over the ice.

"To think that you are here . . ."

"Does it upset you? Does it remind you?"

"Your presence vastly outweighs any bad memories."

Phillip drives expertly, but then again, so does she. Eighteen runs since she began, according to her private logbook. She will not ask him what his various missions have been like, because she already knows.

When they park on the village street, Café Allard presents it-self the way the other shops do: watchful, waiting, invisible unless you know. In the warming temperatures, the sleet has turned to driving rain that has soaked the bottom of her cloak, her shoes. When she returns to her tent, she will clean the shoes and stuff bandages into the toes so that they will retain their shape.

Phillip bangs on a wooden door that has an etched glass win-dow. The design is of a city: Paris, she imagines.

A thin middle-aged man in an apron opens the door.

Phillip asks, in seemingly decent French, if they might have a meal.

"*Mais oui,*" says the man, opening the door wider.

They shake off their wet outerwear and hang it on brass hooks next to a mirror over their table. Etna admires the tattered poster of women dancing, the marble bar with its one unbranded *pres-sion,* the shelf behind the bar covered with exquisitely etched glasses. Their survival intrigues her. She might have come here with other nurses and orderlies any number of times, but she has always begged off, needing rest more than company.

There appears to be only one meal on offer, because the owner has not given them menus. He set before them small glasses of red wine.

"We have the place to ourselves," Phillip says, looking pleased. With his cap off, his hair, dark blond and curly, seems different.

"Your hair used to be straight and combed back off your face."

"The damp," he says. He shrugs and takes a sip of wine.

Etna is anxious about Phillip's survival. She cannot fathom the vitality of this man ever being snuffed out. But she understands the war in a way she has not until now. All those men who died on cots in her tent had cousins, sisters, and friends who cared for them. It seems to her that she and he, in this unimaginable place, are already better known to each other than they were in Thrupp.

The owner brings steaming bowls of stew to the table along with a loaf of bread. They do not ask about the meal, but Phillip drinks in its scent.

"What's in this?" she asks when the owner has left them.

"The French are brilliant at making wonderful meals from the meanest cuts of meat."

Etna savors a spoonful. She tastes meat, yes, but also thyme, carrots, potatoes, and wine. "It's divine."

"We can only hope the recipes survive the Huns." Phillip loosens his tie. Except for his hands and head, he's encased in wool.

"Your accent is British now," she remarks.

"Well, if you remember, I was born in England and lived there until I was ten. I'm tired of being called a Yank."

I'm sure you are, she thinks.

The bread, crusty on the outside, hot on the inside, tastes better than anything Etna has had in months. Perhaps longer. She cannot remember what her family had for meals the previous summer in the States.

"You're very beautiful, you know that?" Phillip says. "I couldn't ever say it to you then, back home, but I can now. You look stronger, more confident."

"Thank you," she says, surprised by his comment.

"You were trapped before. Your face was pinched," he says, trying to explain.

"Was it?"

"Well, not in the cottage. But wary. As if you were listening for footsteps. Were you ever entirely guilt-free living there?"

"Yes, I was." She remembers even now the tremendous sense of freedom and peace she had once she reached the secret cottage and shut the door behind her. "Maybe near the end, when everything went wrong."

"Was the marriage so terrible?"

"I had Clara and Nicky."

"Just so," Phillip says. "I still remember the morning when you came to my family's house to tell Samuel before he left for Canada that you'd broken your engagement to another man."

"That seems so long ago."

The door opens behind Phillip. A British officer and a woman, likely French, enter the café, its windows now beginning to fog. Phillip nods but does not salute. The owner in his white apron appears. The British officer speaks dreadful French. The woman with him must be embarrassed, Etna imagines. Or perhaps she finds it charming.

"I should never have gone to your house," Etna says. "I thought that if Samuel knew I'd broken my engagement..."

"He might stay in Exeter and not go to Canada, where his own fiancée awaited him."

"Yes," she said. "I was out of my mind."

"I've told you this before, but the look on your face that morning is the standard by which I have always measured the ferocity of love."

"Do you still play tennis?" Etna asks to change the subject. She once witnessed Phillip hit a ball clear over the fence into the next yard to settle himself.

Phillip smiles. "Haven't seen a tennis ball in years."

Etna is suddenly curious. "What do you do when you're not driving?"

He sits back and twirls his glass. "If you mean a pastime, I suppose I'd have to say I look for...well...beauty. It sounds ridiculous, but you'd be surprised how difficult it is."

"It doesn't sound ridiculous to me at all."

"It's a humble but challenging quest in this place, a bit like a treasure hunt. When I find something, I note it in a small notebook I carry. Keeps me from going mad, I suppose."

"What have you found?"

He sits back and clears his throat. "I once saw a large flower struggling to poke through the earth. The cracks in the soil caught my attention. I watched the bent stalk pop up as if it were spring-loaded. It was amazing. Let's see." He takes a sip of wine. "I saw a beautiful man, an officer." He pauses, his face somber, perhaps remembering a death. "A field of snow, lit pink. A tooled navy leather journal a soldier kept inside his uniform. He'd barely made two weeks of entries before he was killed. I once watched a priest take ten years off a man's face simply by calming his nerves. Gunfire is beautiful. If you didn't know what it signified, you'd think it was beautiful, too."

"I doubt it. Will you one day write about all this, using your notes?"

He shrugs. "That's not my goal."

"What is your goal?"

"To survive. You?"

"To return to my children."

Phillip nods.

"I asked to be dismissed and was denied."

"Try bereavement. It always works."

"To get me to London, perhaps, but what then?"

"Go to Samuel at the Admiralty. He'll know what to do."

"You know I can't," she says.

Phillip narrows his eyes. "You would put wounded pride before the possibility of returning to your children?"

Chagrined, Etna turns her head away.

"Have you ever been in love, Phillip?" she asks after a time.

He fingers a circle of red wine on the white tablecloth. "I've known love," he says carefully and without explanation.

After Phillip pays the bill, he slips Etna's cloak over her shoulders. "I can get next Saturday night free. Is there a chance you could join me?"

"I'll put in a request. I think they'll grant it because I so seldom go anywhere. The other nurses call me Mother Superior."

Phillip laughs. "I'll come by for you at six, same meeting place. Do you enjoy dancing? I know of a club in Étaples. The drinks are decent. If I don't show up, it doesn't mean I'm dead. It just means I've received unexpected orders."

She gazes through the window at the slanting rain, beginning again to ice up. If only they did not have to leave the little café. "I love dancing," she says.

On Saturday evening, Phillip describes Étaples as he and Etna drive away from the stone barn. "The village was an artists' colony. They came for the incredible light from the sea."

Etna imagines artists in garrets above shops, painting in bright colors, meeting in the evenings with bottles of wine on blue-checked cloths.

"What beautiful thing did you find this week?" she asks.

"I saw a pair of cows behind a whitewashed fence. There were green shoots on the ground. The beauty was in their obliviousness to the insanity around them. They were positively serene."

"You can't have seen green shoots."

"I promise you."

"Will we even know when it's spring?"

"It will rain more."

"I think I may have you beat," Etna says, not without a smile. "I helped a woman give birth. The entire event was beautiful, and the baby girl, when she emerged, had the most wonderful black curls."

"Who was the mother?"

"A French woman who'd walked all the way from her village. She explained that she had nowhere else to go. Soldiers had taken over her house, and it wasn't safe to stay there. Truth be told, we were delighted that she'd come to us. To witness a birth in that place of death and misery . . . even the surgeons couldn't stay away."

"Not all would think a birth beautiful."

"Oh, but it is!" Etna protests.

"Two cows. A baby girl. Both signs of life as it should be. But yes, you win this round."

Pieces of pavement appear to float here and there on the muddy road beneath them. Etna regards her duties in the war as a test of endurance. "We occasionally work twenty-four hours straight," she tells Phillip. "It's not at all unusual to get only four hours of sleep three nights in a row. Sometimes, when I walk into the operating theater, the physicians look more dreadful than the patients."

Phillip concentrates on the road ahead. "My job is a little different. Hours of boredom punctuated by episodes of pure fear. I heard you got caught in the bombardment on Wednesday."

"How did you know?"

"I ask about you."

"Are you trying to look out for me?"

"Something like that," he says and smiles.

During a midmorning return from the aid post, Etna, as part of a three-ambulance convoy, came under bombardment. She chose to leave the road and, for ten or fifteen wild minutes, bounced and careened along the rock-strewn fields before rejoining the convoy, which by then had only one ambulance left—the other having been destroyed.

Officially an adjunct to ambulance unit 3, Etna wears her boots with puttees now, as the men do. Just when she thinks the unit no longer needs her, another driver is wounded or dies. She is always last to be called up, even though a few of the orderlies have told her they would rather be in her truck than with some of the other drivers.

In Étaples, Phillip parks on a back street, the houses dark silhouettes against the moon-sparkle of the Channel.

"I've never been to Étaples," Etna says.

Underground, in the club, the lights dazzle. No wonder men and women take great pains to get here on their nights off. There is a long bar, tables with plum leather chairs, cigarette smoke collecting at the ceiling. Even a small orchestra plays on a stage. Though barely half past six, dancers cover the floor. Most, she guesses, will get only a few hours of sleep before their shifts begin in the morning.

Phillip has on a dress uniform: a British officer-style jacket, white shirt, dark tie, and wide leather belt. In this room of decorated officers, Phillip has little rank. What a waste, she thinks when she remembers his exalted academic reputation. She has to remind herself that he has chosen to be an ambulance driver. That he is a pacifist. The war has been hard on pacifists.

"I can't tell you what's in the drink, except to go easy. A pair of them can make a woman drunk."

"And not a man?" she says teasingly.

"That takes at least three." He presents her with a silver case filled with cigarettes.

"No thank you."

"Do you mind?"

"No, not at all."

Etna has borrowed a dress for the evening, a red gabardine shirtwaist with a ruffled skirt, cut looser than she is used to. How strange that she can have worn, in the past twenty-four hours, the wool skirt of an ambulance driver, the demure headdress of the VAD, and now this red dress that seems to have been made for dancing. "Do you have friends here?"

"Well, none here. Acquaintances, yes. Fortunately, this place isn't exclusive. I'd be thrown out of most clubs officers frequent." He paused. "Would you like to dance?"

Phillip takes her hand and leads her onto the dance floor. He twirls her into a dance embrace.

The orchestra plays "By the Beautiful Sea." Her hand fits smoothly into his. The skirt of the red dress swirls dangerously high when Phillip whips her around.

As the music changes to a ragtime beat and changes again to a melody she's never heard before, Phillip dips her and deftly makes her feel light on her feet. He, so unlike Van Tassel, her former husband, the only man she has intimately touched in years (apart from the wounded), seems completely natural in motion, as if he had been practicing forever. In time, Phillip would have suffocated in Thrupp as the dean of the college, a post her husband now holds.

"Your face is flushed," he says when the music stops.

"I might need to sit this one out."

A woman in a green taffeta dress bends toward the table and asks, "Phil?"

"Marjorie," Phillip answers, standing.

"Introduce me, darling."

"Etna, this is a friend of mine, Marjorie Sherriff."

"Edna, did you say?"

"No, Etna," Phillip repeats.

"Like the mountain," Marjorie muses, assessing whether or not a volcanic mountain is an apt description for the tall woman beside Phillip.

"How do you do?" Etna asks.

"Well, thank you," Marjorie answers, turning away from Etna. "Phil, Jerome is with us. We're at a bigger table. You should join us. Everett and Ruth are here, too. Well, I think Ruth is still with us."

"Do you mind?" Phillip asks Etna.

How can she possibly mind?


All British except for Etna and half of Phillip. Both Marjorie and Ruth, who just manages to sit upright, are nurses with the British Expeditionary Force. The two men drive ambulances, which explains how they know Phillip.

"Another Yank," says Jerome. "You're at Camiers."

"Yes, I am."

"Heroes," he tells the table. "Not even in the war, and still they volunteer."

"Nothing heroic about it," Etna says.

The hairstyles of the two women fascinate Etna. Ruth, a brunette, has bobbed her hair, the curls falling above her shoulders. It's a smart look, somewhat ruined by her sodden eyes. Marjorie, who is blond, has her hair crimped and pulled back.

*Darling.*

Jerome, his face full of freckles, stretches his body beneath the table. Everett has long brown hair slicked back from a high fore-head. Everyone except Etna smokes.

"You got caught in the bombardment," Jerome says, address-ing Etna.

"I did, yes."

"The way I heard it," he says to the table, "she executed a per-fect shortcut through the fields."

"Just for a minute or two."

"You saved your wounded. That's the kind of thing they give medals for."

"They give medals to ambulance drivers?" she asks unthinkin-gly, and then covers her blunder by saying, "I should hope they'd give a medal to the ambulance driver who stayed on the road and made it safely to camp."

"I don't know," says Jerome, determined to give her a compli-ment. "Quick wits on your part."

Merely the will to live, she wants to say.

Phillip puts his arm around her shoulders, and she understands it as a protective gesture.

A meal arrives of unidentifiable fish in a white sauce. Bottles of wine appear on the table. Ruth seems to have fallen asleep.

"Is she all right?" Etna asks.

"She shouldn't drink," Everett says. "In fact, I ought to drive her back."

"You can't take her back in that condition," protests Marjorie. "Besides, I would have to leave, too, and I'm not ready. Find some of that brew they're calling coffee now, get it into her, and walk her around outside. She's got to be able to walk into her tent. I can't very well carry her."

Everett does as he is told, which leaves only the four of them. Marjorie shows no sign of tiring. She asks Phillip to dance. He hesitates, perhaps not wanting to leave Etna alone. Can Marjorie be the person to whom Phillip was referring when he said he had known love?

Well mannered, Jerome asks Etna if she would like to dance.

"If you don't mind, I'd rather sit a moment."

"Me, too," Jerome says with relief. "She's wearing me out."

Etna smiles.

"We're all a bit in awe of you," Jerome confesses.

"Why so?"

"You've taken on the double role of VAD and ambulance driver. Not sure I've ever met anyone who answers to that description."

"The war has caused all of us to be people we didn't used to be."

"Isn't that the truth." Jerome picks up a bottle of wine and offers to pour some into her glass. She shakes her head no.

"What were you before the war?" she asks.

"Librarian."

"You must miss your books," she says.

"I've got a copy of *Paradise Lost* on onionskin in tiny print. My mother gave it to me before I left. I've read it nine times."

"You should have a new book."

"Most of the men in the corps don't care much for reading."

"Surely Phillip—"

"No, that's odd, he being an academic and all. He seems to have no interest in books."

"I'm very surprised," Etna says.

Phillip appears with Marjorie, who clings to him. Etna has forgotten to watch the pair dancing.

"I'd best be getting you back," Phillip says to Etna.

"Must you?" A whine from Marjorie.

"I have to get up early," Etna says.

"Lovely to meet you," Marjorie offers in a bored voice, not even bothering to look at Etna. A languid dismissal.

"Was that so terrible?" Phillip asks when they have found his vehicle.

"Oh, not at all. I quite enjoyed the dancing and even talking to Jerome."

"He's lost two brothers already. He's the only son left. They ought to send him home."

"But they won't?"

"Don't think so."

Etna can see the mother: benumbed, quiet, getting on with life for the sake of Jerome. Not for her husband, whom she barely notices. He with his own grief. Two sons, two extreme sacrifices, too much for anyone to bear.

"The attrition is beyond anything the generals can have imagined," Phillip points out. "Certainly they couldn't have anticipated such large numbers of British dead."

"Jerome and I got into the subject of books," Etna says. "He mentioned that you no longer read."

"No. Not at the moment."

When they reach the stone barn, Phillip turns in his seat to face her. "You'll never guess what I've found."

He smiles, and she can't help but smile with him. "What?"

"A tennis court."

"Never."

"I did. A clay court belonging to an abandoned château."

"It's February."

"Almost March. We'll get a dry spell."

"Where will you find a tennis ball and rackets?"

"I don't know, but I will," he says. "I have to restore my reputation."

He hops down from the truck and comes around to Etna's side.

"I had a lovely evening," she says as he opens the door.

"So did I." He takes her hand.

For a moment, she thinks he will pull her into a dance move. He bends and kisses her hand instead, a courtly gesture. Impulsively, she embraces him.

She stands back. "Was that all right?"

"I adore you, Etna. I always have."

She slips her hand from his and walks away from the truck.

The quest for beautiful moments challenges Etna as February moves closer to March. The relentless rain turns everything unpaved into a pool of mud. During the months Etna has been driving an ambulance, she has learned basic maintenance. She can change a tire, check the oil, fill a radiator, and adjust a clutch. Despite this additional knowledge, the actual managing of the truck has become more difficult. The mud sucks in anything with weight. She uses thin metal wedges to dig into the muck under the front of the rear tires. With the wedges, an orderly pushing, and a gentle rocking motion, Etna learns how to gun her ambulance out of the bog. She invents grassy routes and even routes that traverse tufts in fields. With careful steering, she can maneuver the truck onto drier land, a process not unlike stepping across stones to reach the other side of a rushing stream.

Etna finds a lost brooch near the Regimental Aid Post. It puzzles her, even after she turns it in. What is a ruby-and-gold pin doing in a world peopled entirely by men? Can another female driver have had it pinned to her underthings? Can a soldier have lost a prized gift from his sweetheart? When she turns it in to an officer, neither he nor anyone else seems to have much use for it, rubies being of little currency in the trenches. In the end, she decides she cannot count the brooch, though attractive, as something beautiful.

She does see, however, a gold cross on a gold chain tucked into the hollow of a man's clavicle. The bright gold on the soldier's white skin, the muscles beneath it smooth and broad, moves her. A mother, a sister, a wife gave the man the cross, believing that the religious symbol would protect him. But before the aides have finished undressing him, a priest has to be summoned.

One afternoon, following heavy rain and a brief clearing, a rainbow appears. It seems to start south of Camiers and end somewhere near the front, where surely no pot of gold awaits. An illusion, and a common one at that, the rainbow summons grown men from the tents. They watch in silence as the rainbow disappears.

Phillip picks her up at the stone barn in early March. Each of them has time only for a quick drink and perhaps a bite of bread before they have to return to duty.

"You go first," she says, staring at his face as he backs up his ambulance. He executes the turn and bounces off the road. He, too, has invented his own grassy route to the village.

"I came across a driver who had made for himself a sort of tea service that he kept in his kit," he began. "One day, when we were bored, he showed it to me. He'd invented a collapsible tin cup with sliding sides and a partially detachable bottom. His teapot was made of tin also, and when I first saw it, it looked like a flat disk with two other disks attached. It worked like the cup, except that it had a sealed top with a small hole in it. He had tea in tiny hand-sewn silk bags and small paper packets of dried milk. No sugar, of course. I asked if he could make me a cup, and he said he would. He had with him a short flat candle with a wick. When the small teapot was held against the flame, the water heated surprisingly quickly. Of course, it produced only the one cup, which was hard to touch without gloves, but I have to say it was the best cup of tea I think I've ever had."

"Ingenious," Etna says. "I think we'll have to let that count as two beautiful things. The design of the equipment and the taste of the tea. Anything beautiful counts, yes? Taste? Scent?"

"And you?"

Etna tells him of the rainbow and the cross. "I haven't ruined it for you, have I? Making your pastime a game?"

"Not at all. I'm highly competitive."

The owner nods as they enter the café. Once again, they find themselves alone because of the hour, four o'clock in the afternoon. Phillip speaks to the waiter, who brings two delicate glasses of transparent gold liquid and, with them, a pitcher of water, a packet containing a few miraculous grains of sugar, and two cups of tea.

"I was famished for tea after my story," Phillip says. "The drink is Pernod. You put some water in—like this—and a little sugar." Etna watches as the drink turns a milky custard yellow. "Tastes a bit like aniseed. It's been a rough couple of weeks for me, and I imagine for you, too. This muck is much worse than the ice."

She takes a sip of the yellow liquid. "Phillip, we'd better see to that tennis game fairly soon."

"In this mess?"

"I've got a week's leave March thirteenth."

He must have known it was coming, but still he seems startled by the news.

"I'm happy for you," he says after a time. "You'll go to London first?"

"Yes, and I will look Samuel up. It's the only thing I can think of."

"I'm sure he'll be happy to help. He owes you."

"No, no, he doesn't, Phillip. From his point of view, he did the only possible thing. He has a wife and children now. I assume he's happy."

"With the children, yes. I can't say the marriage is a happy one."

"I'm sorry to hear that," Etna says.

"So was I. We didn't speak for years, but I never wished him an unhappy life. I think it's why he was so willing to go to London."

"Wasn't he ordered to?"

"He was invited to. It's a little different. He could have found commensurate work in Halifax. I went to see him when I first got to London. He was furious with me for having left America and even angrier when I told him I intended to go to France. We had a row. A big one. I tell you this because you might not want to mention me."

"Phillip, are you unhappy?" Etna asks.

He seems surprised by the question. "Not particularly."

"Sometimes you seem...I don't know if *remote* is the word. *Guarded,* I would say."

His gray eyes meet hers. He shrugs. "If we get four good days in a row, I'll come get you."

Etna backtracks as well. "Did you find rackets and a ball?"

"I did. In Étaples. I asked a boy if he knew where I could get hold of the equipment, and the next day he sold me his. I suspect it may have belonged to his father. Are you sorry you came here?"

"I may be in the future," she says. "But I'm not now. I know I've done something good, and I've learned a little about myself."

"What's that?"

"I'm useful here."


On the fifth of March, the sun finally emerges and seems likely to stay. The sight of it, the warmth of it, raises everyone's spirits, even those of the wounded. Etna, who used to find sunny days painful, revels in the light. She begins to count the days.

On the fourth successive good day, she waits for a message. When none comes, she begins to wonder if Phillip has forgotten his promise. But in the first post of the fifth day, there is a letter.

*Find a way. I'll be there at twelve thirty. P.*

The grippe, she tells the ward sister, who looks her over and then dismisses her with a wave. Etna must stay in uniform, lest she be seen walking from the tent or coming back later in the afternoon in civilian clothes. At the appointed time, she follows her usual route. Most days, the nurses do not have time to check on one of their own until after the evening meal. If they find Etna missing, she will simply say that the symptoms of her illness kept her in the privy most of the day.

Phillip is waiting for her. She climbs quickly into the passenger seat.

"That was nerve-racking," she says.

"What did you say to get the time off?"

"I'm sick with the grippe."

"Don't give it to me."

Because the road is full of dried ruts, the truck bounces violently from side to side. Still, ruts are better than muck. When they are half a mile from the field hospital, Etna relaxes into the pure pleasure of escaping the camp with an entire afternoon of warm sunshine ahead of her. She whips off her cap, takes out her pins, and lets her hair go free in the wind made by the truck. "Phillip, this is just the best present."

"Present? I intend to wallop you."

As they drive, Etna notices red veils of buds in the forest. She inhales the clean air. They take a turn and seem to be driving inland. From the nature of the roads, not rutted, she guesses they have not been traveled much.

"Do you do this often? Go for rides in the afternoon?"

"Not often. The ambulances are always needed, and I have to be careful about petrol. On the day I found the château, I was on a supply mission."

The woods open up to vast fields. When they pass an orchard, Etna marvels at the dark pink cherry buds. Acres of them. "How have these survived?" she asks Phillip.

"Oh, they'll be decimated, too, I shouldn't wonder. Hopefully not before they bear fruit."

"What will happen to us if we're caught?"

"Well, if we're caught by our side, I might get some lashes, hard labor." He does not mention what would happen if they were to be caught by the Germans. "What about you?"

"I have no idea. A severe reprimand. But no punishment, I think. What on earth would they punish me with? The head nurse needs my hands too much."

"I suppose I could be sent to the front line. Make an example of the conchie."

"They wouldn't."

The top of a stone structure rises above the trees in the distance. "Is that it?" Etna asks.

Phillip nods.

"And it's really abandoned?"

"Yes."

"And not been requisitioned?"

"Apparently not."

"How amazing."

As they draw closer, Etna studies the gray stone building, magnificent and austere. The windows above the ground floor are narrow and long, the two turrets imposing.

"Years ago, this must have been a fortress," Phillip says. "Hence the stingy windows. Big enough to see out of, but not big enough to penetrate from the outside. This house might be three hundred years old. Hard to say. My French architecture is a bit rusty."

Only on the ground floor does the house resemble a grand and welcoming residence. Large square windows with beveled panes flank the massive wooden door.

Phillip parks the truck around the back of the château, though it hardly matters. They cannot be seen from the road. "When I drove in here the first time, I was certain someone would start shooting. If you listen, though, the only thing you can hear is birds."

Etna steps out. No guns, no screams, no noisy vehicles. The grounds slope away from the château so that it sits on a promontory. All around them are open fields, overgrown gardens, orchards, and, to one side, what looks to be an old tennis court. "That's it," she says.

"If you carry the ball and the rackets, I'll get the picnic."

"Picnic?"

"I made a trip into the village to see our friend Monsieur Allard. He gave me bread and cheese and a bottle of wine."

"Wine. We'll get tipsy," she says. "You'll beat me."

"I'm going to beat you anyway, so you might as well enjoy yourself."

Phillip leads them down the hill to the court. The net droops to the ground. Irregular holes have been torn in the fencing. When Etna steps onto the clay, she finds that it is spongy in parts. The trick will be to deaden the ball by landing it in one of these spots, or to learn where the dry ground is in order to bounce it past Phillip. At best, the game will be comical.

"I see you've got only the one ball," Etna says as she walks to the serving line.

"Couldn't find another."

"Then you'd better not hit it over the fence this time," she says with a wink.

Phillip laughs. He removes his brown wool tunic to reveal only an undershirt beneath. She takes off her apron. They hang their clothes from openings in the fence. Etna pins her hair back up.

"Anytime," Phillip says.

She serves the ball, and though she has done so badly, it hits a wet spot and dies before Phillip can even get to it.

Etna laughs. "I'll try it again."

"No, that was a proper serve. Point to you."

"If you give away points like that, you'll never win."

"Do I look worried?"

When Phillip serves, the ball hits dry ground and spins away from Etna. A proper point.

He does it again, and then a third time.

"Have you been out here surveying the court?" she asks.

First game to Phillip. Second to Etna when she breaks his serve.

From a not-quite-deadening patch of clay, Phillip's return hits the top of the net and stays there. The two of them wait for the ball to drop, but the slackening leather has created a perfect pocket. They walk toward the net to examine the situation. "Point to you," Phillip concedes, wiping sweat from his brow with the back of his hand.

"No, I couldn't possibly," Etna says.

"Let's take a break. We'll have some water and then our lunch with a little wine. By the time we're done, the wind will have knocked it one way or the other."

Etna welcomes the respite. Despite the physical demands of her job, she is not in good condition for sports.

They both tumble onto the grass of a gentle slope. "Do you mind if I don't put that wretched tunic back on?" Phillip asks.

"Not at all," she says, aware of his naked arms and the muscles of his chest under the now nearly transparent undershirt. They pass his canteen back and forth. "Best to leave a bit for later," he advises. She watches as he opens his rucksack and brings out some cheese wrapped in paper, a loaf of bread, and a bottle of wine. Allard has opened the wine and recorked it for Phillip. He arranges their repast on the metal plate from his kit. He puts a knife into the cheese. "Ladies first," he says, gesturing.

The delicate cheese atop a crusty piece of bread seems like a promise from a world she barely knows. They share a tin cup of the wine. The meal feels, in its simplicity and on that hillside, vaguely biblical.

"You'd think we'd never seen food before," she says when they have devoured almost all the cheese and bread. She flops back onto the grass, arms behind her head. "I'm going to need a few minutes before I get up again."

Phillip lounges on his side, facing Etna.

"This is lovely," she says. "So perfect. Thank you."

"I'm rather enjoying this myself." He is ahead in points, though should the ball drop onto his side, Etna will be in a position to continue the game.

"I think I'm drunk," Etna says.

"Nonsense. You're tipsy."

"Is there a difference?"

"Oh, yes. You've probably never encountered a real drunk before. Even if they're close to death, they don't get sent on to the hospitals. The men *wishing* they were dead are never treated. They're just left to suffer."

"You've been drunk?"

"Of course. No proper man hasn't."

She stares at the pillow clouds the way she used to as a child. "Phillip, what was it like for you in Thrupp? Do you mind my asking?"

"Here? You can ask me anything you want."

"Was it hard?"

"Yes. I'd studied for years to attain my position at Yale. My mistake was allowing myself to be seduced by the notion of becoming head of Thrupp."

"You were cajoled into the post by the board of corporators."

"Perhaps. But I had ambition, too. The idea of being dean was heady."

"In such a backwater place?"

"That was the point, you see. I felt I could improve Thrupp, give Dartmouth a run for its money. That was the challenge I couldn't resist—to be able to steer the school in an enlightened direction. I should have left immediately after the lectures were finished."

"And you regret it."

"Yes. Who in his right mind would choose the trenches of France over the Gothic passageways of Yale?"

"And when Nicholas told everyone of your supposed advances toward Clara?"

"At first I laughed it off," he says. "I couldn't believe it. When I realized the college and the police were taking the charges seriously, I was sick at heart. I was ruined, yes, but it was worse than that. It was being implicated in any way in Professor Van Tassel's cruelty to the child that sickened me."

A sound pricks Etna's ear. She waits a few seconds to determine its origin. When she does, she puts a hand on Phillip's arm. He looks down at the place where she is touching him, up at her, and then he hears it, too.

He nods. The sound of a motor.

Remaining as low as he can, he stuffs everything into his sack. With that and the rackets, he runs, crouched, to his tunic while Etna retrieves her apron. Phillip signals to her to follow him as he heads straight for the woods not thirty feet from the court. The sound of the motor grows louder until a sleek midnight-blue touring car pulls into the circular drive. A chauffeur stays in the vehicle while a man in civilian clothes gets out and bangs on the front door of the château.

The gentleman, well dressed and wearing a top hat, stands back from the doorway and then peers into each window of the front of the house. He turns the corner to examine the side of the house Etna and Phillip cannot see. The unknown trespasser walks in their direction, giving a quick glance down the side of the hill. With his hands on his hips, he seems to stare straight at them. He remains in this position for what feels like hours. From the way he turns his head back and forth, Etna deduces he is not searching for something or someone but rather examining the property. Does he want to buy the place? She hopes he is not thorough enough to inspect the tennis court. If he does, will he notice their recent footsteps and the ball caught on the net? She imagines the man to be French, too old, perhaps, to have been called up to fight. Or possibly he scouts houses for the French army to use as headquarters. The ambulance parked out back would raise suspicions and might require a broader search.

"You ought to breathe," Phillip whispers to Etna.

She stays in her crouched position, one hand on the ground steadying herself, the other clutching the white apron in such a way that the red cross does not show.

Abruptly, the man pivots, walks to the touring car, and slides in. The car continues on the circular driveway and then out the way it came.

Etna bows her head.

"That was close," Phillip says.

"Who do you think he was?"

"He could be anything from an old friend visiting to a German spy getting the lay of the land. I couldn't determine the make of the motorcar."

"What do we do now?" Etna whispers.

"Sit here for ten minutes. Go through the woods until we're behind the house. Make a run for it to the truck and get the hell out of here."

"We'll never know which way the ball went," Etna says, unable to see the court from where they are.

"Just as well. You're much too competitive."

"Why are we whispering?"

Phillip laughs. "I don't know. This feels transgressive."

"It is."

They wait ten minutes by Phillip's tin watch. "Follow me," he says. He plunges ahead, frequently turning to look for Etna. When they reach the back of the house, they move slowly out to the clearing. The slope is steeper in the back than it was at the side of the house.

"You ready?" Phillip asks Etna. "I think we should run. We're far later than I thought."

"I'll try."

They scramble up the hill, sometimes upright, sometimes crouched, Etna falling behind Phillip. He waits for her to catch up, but she's breathless. "You go on," she gasps, pointing to the truck. "Don't stand here. Go."

When she finally reaches the truck, the sun is setting, and the chill dries the sweat from her body.

"You strike me as a woman crawling for independence."

"Not running?"

"I'm not sure the world will allow that right now."

"Your cheeks are red, and you seem much better," the ward sister notes when Etna makes her appearance in the hospital tent.

The next morning, on March 11, Etna and her colleagues are woken by a fierce bombardment at dawn. The field hospital braces for an increased number of casualties. Etna moves quickly, making beds, pouring glasses of water, folding bandages, and counting basins. She also numbers the syringes of morphine at the ready.

A convoy of five ambulances drives in sooner than the team expected them. Stretcher bearers scatter throughout the tents with the wounded. The proportion of seriously injured to merely wounded is larger than Etna has ever seen before. The nurses and orderlies immediately begin cutting away uniforms, removing makeshift dressings, and bathing the wounded. In the theaters, surgeons work like butchers. Etna moves along the aisles, glancing from side to side, assessing what each man will need. In doing so, she passes a terrifying human being. The man has no face, the worst of all injuries. Despite her self-discipline, she shudders. She can hardly bear to gaze upon him. She moves on, but a sound like a grunt follows her. Not a word, but a communication.

She turns and walks back to the bed. She bends over.

*Always look the wounded in the eye,* she has been taught.

Etna's head fills with harsh noise. Her torso hollows out.

She knows by the good eye, which follows hers. She knows by the shape of his beautiful head.

She tries to speak, but no words come. No words of endearment or friendship or of comfort. Syllables and sentences can never compensate for the terrible chain of events that has resulted in this ravaged face.

An orderly drapes a sterile cloth over the man's injuries. "Nurse, you're needed elsewhere," he instructs.

"I know this man," Etna says.

"Worse luck you."

"I can't leave him."

"Poor sod."

"He can hear you," she says through clenched teeth.

"It isn't anything he doesn't already know," the orderly says and leaves.

Etna falls to her knees. She puts her mouth near Phillip's ear. "I am with you," she says as she clutches his hand. "I am with you."

The ward sister touches her shoulder. "This one's tapped for surgery," she announces.

*This one.*

"Be careful," Etna calls. The orderlies walk quickly to an operating theater. She runs with them, trying to keep her hand on the stretcher. She does this until a surgeon demands that she leave.

She stumbles from the tent to a day splendid with sunshine.

She falls, her knees and hands in the dirt. No one notices the aide on all fours.

"Oh, God, oh, God, oh, God," she cries.

After a time, she pulls herself upright and begins to walk toward the perimeter. When she reaches the woods, she moves through them, furiously pushing away the scratchy branches. At the stone barn, where she and Phillip used to meet, she runs screaming into an open field.

*America, February 1917*

En route to America
February 20, 1917

My dear Dr. Bridge,

Directly after hearing my true name in the Admiralty,
Captain Samuel Asher, whom I once knew, took me to
stay with his sister, Elinor, in Minerva Mews. I regret that
I wasn't able to say good-bye to you in person. In the
middle of the third night, I was awakened and rushed to
Southampton, where I boarded a ship of diplomats headed
for America. I could not tolerate the thought of another day
passing with you not knowing where I was, and so I gave Samuel two letters to post for me: one to you and one to Lily.
In hers, I explained my situation and thanked her for her
extraordinary hospitality. I wished her well in her months
ahead and told her I hope for a photograph when the baby
is christened.

As for you, Dr. Bridge, my gratitude is enormous. I have
come to trust you in a way I doubt I shall ever trust anyone
again. You gave me attention when you could ill afford the
time to do it. Had it not been for you, I wouldn't have been

prepared for the moment when I realized I was not who I thought I was.

Regarding our treatment sessions, I am sorry to report that the ailments that plagued me have not entirely gone away. The pains in my legs have returned on two separate occasions, which no one witnessed. Their return upsets me even more now than it did before, for I fear there will never be a cure. I'm wondering if I ought to seek out the advice of a doctor when I arrive in America. I rely on you to tell me what to do.

I hope you will not think me too bold, but I feel that it is only fair to you to explain the history behind the drawings you spent so much time studying. The man I drew on the blanket with the telescope is, in fact, the very same Captain Samuel Asher you met at the Admiralty. It was he who said my name. He and I were young lovers. Eventually, he married and left Exeter, New Hampshire, for Toronto, where his wife's family lived and where he taught physics. Whatever was between us ended quite some time ago, and he was nothing but kind to me while I resided with his sister.

The drawing of the man in the bed is of my husband, Nicholas Van Tassel, a man I never loved. On one occasion in August of 1915, he attacked me, which was the prime reason I left the country soon afterward.

Phillip Asher, younger brother of Samuel, is the half face I drew. A driver with the ambulance corps, he was a good friend to me when I served in Camiers. On March 11 of last year, he was horribly injured. He is still undergoing surgeries to repair his face. Phillip had been a visiting academic in Thrupp, where I lived with my husband, also a professor. In competition with Phillip for the post of dean of Thrupp College, my husband managed to ruin Phillip's distinguished reputation and create the most heinous of scandals around him. Phillip left America and immediately joined the war in France. I tried to find him there and persuade him to return to America. After I saw Phillip's injured face in the hospital tent in Camiers, I fled into the fields, believing that my family, specifically my husband, had caused this second ruination of a decent man. That is all I remember until I woke two days later in a hospital in Marne. You know the rest.

You will perhaps have guessed by now that the garden I drew represented the one I had at home in Thrupp, New Hampshire, and that the presence I felt in it was my children, Clara, now sixteen, and Nicky, now eight. And as for the cottage I drew with the menacing trees outside the windows, it remained for a time a secret oasis that I purchased without my husband's knowledge. It was there that I began sketching in earnest.

The terrible thing I once confessed to you I felt I had done was my abandonment of my children when I was not in my right mind. I go now to find them again.

Though I left in haste, I have never stopped thinking of you and your gift to me.

With great affection,

Etna

En route to America,
February 20, 1917

Dear Samuel,

I want to say again how grateful I am to you and your sister for taking me in and arranging passage to America. I will, as soon as I have employment, pay you in full for the ticket.

I appreciated your silence on the matter of our earlier romance—I can think of no other way to put it. The several days I spent with Elinor were fragile ones for me, and I had all I could do to sort out my nearer past.

I cannot pretend to know your thoughts, but if you have felt the tiniest distress about the way our earlier relationship ended, you must not. My time with you remains a sweet memory. I used to think I would hold on to my feelings for you forever, but the years and the difficult experiences I have had since then have muted them as if they were voices from my childhood.

I wish you well in your further responsibilities. It is rumored that America will soon enter the war. We all hope for a speedy end to that terrible conflict.

With gratitude,

Etna

Bryanston Square,
London, England
19 March 1917

Dear Etna,

I was greatly relieved to receive your letter. I did know that you had set sail for America because I went round to Captain Asher's office and spoke with him, and though I was, I confess, hurt that you had not said good-bye to me and Lily (I can see from your letter that you could not), I was glad to know that you were en route to your children, and even happier when later I received a marconigram from Asher telling me that you had safely reached your destination.

The hospital where Phillip Asher resides is also a nursing home where he can live with other men with similar injuries. Phillip is progressing well, I am told.

Lily is thriving and gives you her best wishes for a happy reunion with your children.

May I just say that witnessing your physical transformation at the Admiralty when you learned of your identity was one of the most astonishing sights of my life. Though you were highly distressed, your back straightened and the features of your face became more defined, as if the prescription of my spectacles had been changed. It was clear that Stella Bain had gone and Etna Bliss had come alive.

I think often of Stella Bain, the woman who struggled with so much.

Fondly, as always,

August Bridge

Gainesville, Florida
March 20, 1917

Dear August,

I write to tell you that I have been reunited with my daughter, Clara. The reunion requires a long letter, which I will try to write before the end of the week. I will soon travel to New Hampshire to see my son, Nicky. I face a battle ahead, for I will fight for custody of them, but I wanted you especially to know this happy news, which I hope you will share with Lily.

With affection,
Etna

Bryanston Square
London, England
9 June 1917

Dear Etna,

I must give you the sad news that Lily died yesterday at nine twenty-three in the morning. Despite the best efforts of the surgeon and the midwife, Lily bled to death as a result of her labor having begun too early, thus rupturing the placenta before emergency procedures could begin. I was, however, able to save the infant, a boy, whom I will call Sebastian.

I cannot say any more.

August

Gainesville, Florida
June 21, 1917

Dear August,

Your news about Lily has left me in mourning for her lovely person, for the life that might have been, and for the life that once was yours.

That you should spend your days as a firsthand witness to such destruction and death and then have to suffer the loss of your wife in a place where she was meant to be safe is too bitter an irony to bear. My constant sympathy is with you.

I know that you and Sebastian will find joy in each other.

With the greatest sorrow and affection,

Etna

Bryanston Square
London, England
21 July 1917

Dear Etna,

It has been more than a month since Lily died, and I have
been unable to write or to read a word until today. Lily was
buried in her family plot in Greenwich. I refuse the Victorian
method of grieving and the over-sanctifying of death. It is
with us; it is a part of life. Though I, a physician, should have
been prepared, I thought the universe—at least at home—to
be a kinder one. I think of the thousands of mothers and wives
whose clock has stopped in 1917. Mine has, too.

Though I have hired a nanny, I spend as much time as I am
able with Sebastian every day. I love to hold him in my arms.

I continue to take my daily stroll through the Bryanston
Square garden. That and my time with Sebastian are my
only diversions. That the world should go about its cy-
cles—the garden is awash in roses—strikes me this year as
not the miracle I have always felt it to be, but rather an in-
sult to those of us who still reside in a place called winter.

As ever,

August

*New Hampshire, March 1918*

So there is to be a trial.

"I hope you will not mind my saying this, Mrs. Van Tassel, but you have a difficult case before you."

"I understand."

Averill Hastings is the third lawyer Etna has consulted. The first two, after investigating her petition, refused her.

"As I wrote to you, the judge has agreed to go forward with your petition, even though your husband will not divorce you. Indeed, it is because of Mr. Van Tassel's obstinacy that the judge sees no other way to ensure your right to be a parent to your son. There is precedent for this."

"I am most grateful."

If this is not Mr. Hastings's first trial, it must surely be his second. The new lawyer, painfully thin, cannot be older than twenty-five. His suit hangs on narrow shoulders, and his fingers tremble as he writes in a notebook. His pinched mouth and his close-set eyes do not add to his handsomeness, and she fears he will not be a robust presence in front of the judge.

"Will Mr. Van Tassel be present in the courtroom?" Etna asks, noting the apprehension in her voice, an apprehension she will have to rid herself of before the hearing.

"It is hard to say at this time. Some courts favor the presence of the Respondent. Others do not. If you do not mind, Mrs. Van

Tassel, I have some questions I should like to ask you. These are so I may be prepared as best I can."

"Yes, certainly," Etna says.

"Where were you born?"

"In Exeter, New Hampshire."

"In what year."

"In 1876."

"So you are..."

"Forty-one. Forty-two in August."

"And how old were you when you met and married Nicholas Van Tassel?"

"I was twenty-three when I met him and twenty-four when I married him."

"At twenty-three years of age, how were you keeping yourself?"

"I had, some months before coming to Thrupp to stay with my aunt and uncle, lost whatever means I might have had from the family estate upon the death of my mother. My sister, Miriam, and her husband gained control not only of the house but also of whatever funds remained."

"And you were left with nothing?"

"Does this have bearing on the case at hand?" Etna asks.

"It may," Mr. Hastings responds, regarding her carefully. "If you were penniless at the time you agreed to marry Mr. Van Tassel, it may help to explain why you entered into a marriage with a man who was perhaps not best suited for you."

Maybe Averill Hastings is shrewder than Etna has previously given him credit for.

"You and your husband lived together for fifteen years."

"Yes."

"And how would you characterize this marriage?"

How is she to answer this question? The marriage was different minute to minute, as are all marriages, she suspects, and yet maddeningly the same day after day. Until the end. Until the unbearable end.

"We had respect for one another," she says, deciding even as she answers him that she must tell the lawyer the truth about the marriage if he is to properly represent her. "But there was great unhappiness on my part. You see, I married Mr. Van Tassel because I had sympathy for him, not because I loved him." And that was the original sin, she thinks now, from which came all that happened later.

"Can you explain?"

"In 1899, he became, I suppose you would say, obsessed with me. If that sounds overly self-regarding, I apologize. I suspected that one day he would propose to me, and when he did, I turned him down, as I did not love him."

"If you did not love him, how was the man encouraged to propose to you? I assume you had walked out with him?"

"Yes," Etna says, remembering the stifling atmosphere of her aunt and uncle's house in Thrupp, her desperate desire to be out of doors, even on the coldest of days, and how she happened to meet Professor Van Tassel during a hotel fire. He offered her the very thing she craved: a chance to be away from the house. What irony that she should have been with him so that she could breathe, and yet she was always short of breath in his presence. "I suppose you could say that I used him to get away from rather stifling living conditions."

"No, you will not say that," Mr. Hastings quickly informs her. "You will not say that you used him. And I am quite certain that you are misstating the case. You have mentioned that he pursued you in an obsessive fashion."

"Yes."

"And that you refused to marry him."

"Yes. After that refusal, I left Thrupp to go live with my sister and her husband in Exeter."

"In what used to be your own home."

"Yes."

"And what was your position in your sister's house?"

"I went to visit so that I might get away from Mr. Van Tassel, but it soon became clear to me that I had my room and board in exchange for being governess to my sister's children."

"Indeed. Did that strike you as degrading or attractive?"

"Not necessarily degrading, but it was not a life I wanted for myself."

"So if you accepted that proposition, you would have again entrapped yourself?"

"My sister and I were never close."

"Mr. Van Tassel must have approached you again about marriage."

"Yes. He came to Exeter some weeks after I had arrived there. When we had an opportunity to speak alone, I saw genuine love and hope and promise in his face, and in that moment, I pitied him."

"You pitied him."

"Yes. I agreed to his proposal."

Mr. Hastings flips a page of his notebook. Etna notices that his little finger and the side of his writing hand are stained with black ink.

"How old were you when you had Clara?"

"I was twenty-five."

"And Nicodemus?"

"I had several miscarriages," she says and immediately sees a purplish color flood Mr. Hastings's face. Is he embarrassed, or has she become so used to the functions and parts of the body that she is too free with her descriptions? "Nicky was born when I was thirty-three."

"How would you characterize your relationship with your children?"

"I loved them with all my heart."

"Mrs. Van Tassel, I think it would be better to say, 'I *love* them with all my heart.'"

"Yes, definitely."

"Can you be more specific?"

"I was very involved in their daily lives. I played with them. I corrected their behavior. I tutored them in lessons. I inspired in them a love of the outdoors with outdoor games. They became very interested in our garden."

"And I assume you took them to Sunday school regularly."

Etna does not respond immediately, because she understands the import of the question. She and Van Tassel nominally belonged to the First Congregational Church, but she cannot say she regularly took her children to church or to Sunday school.

"Mrs. Van Tassel?"

"I took the children to church, but not regularly."

Mr. Hastings's left eyebrow rises.

"Will that be a problem?"

"I think you will say that you took your children to church and leave it at that and hope that the inquiry ends there. If Mr. Van Tassel is in the courtroom, will he tell his lawyer to query you further on this?"

"He had little interest in church, either, so I think he will say nothing. When we are at the hearing, I suggest you address him as Dean Van Tassel, since he is likely to bristle at a simple 'Mister.'"

"Good point. Thank you. Mrs. Van Tassel, were your children aware that there was no love on your part toward your husband during the marriage?"

"I cannot say for sure."

"May I guide your answer? If you are not sure, you must, of course, say so. But a better answer might be, 'I saw nothing in their behavior that would indicate that.'"

"My husband and I were not overly affectionate with each other in their presence, but we did not argue, either. We were affectionate with the children in each other's presence. I think other parents behave the same way."

*Or do they?* Etna wonders now. Might an astute daughter of thirteen years have wondered why her mother seldom laughed with her father?

"Mrs. Van Tassel," Averill Hastings asks, "have you *seen* your children?"

"Oh, yes," Etna says to the lawyer. "I have seen my children."

When Etna arrived at her hotel in Gainesville, after an arduous journey by sea and by train, she sent a note to Meritable Root, her sister-in-law, who had been taking care of Clara since Etna had fled the house in 1915. Meritable replied that she would meet Etna for tea in the hotel lobby at four o'clock.

Etna was in the lobby early and had a chance to watch the stout Meritable be helped from her motorcar. Her sister-in-law did not resemble Van Tassel at all in personality—being the mother of eleven children, she had a simple, jovial manner about her—but the physical resemblance to Etna's hated husband was still evident.

Meritable took Etna's hand, as a woman will, a clasp and not a shake. Etna helped her sit, because Meritable seemed to be out of breath. After they had exchanged pleasantries and ordered tea, Meritable talked about Clara.

"This will hurt you, Etna, but I must tell you that she rarely speaks of you. One of the reasons is that we told her you had gone away for your health, that it was necessary for you to have complete rest in order to fully recuperate. She asked us what your ailment was, and we told her it was a kind of exhaustion only rest could cure. One other time, about six months ago, when Clara and Henry were out riding, she asked him if her mother would ever get better. Henry replied it was just a matter of time. So you see, Etna, it will not be as difficult as it might be for us to inform her that you are now well and have come to see her."

"She'll be upset," Etna said, still shaken by the news that her daughter rarely spoke of her.

"Maybe, but she is a strong girl."

Etna asked how best to approach the meeting of mother and daughter. Meritable said she would speak privately with Clara first and set a time and day on the weekend—perhaps the following Sunday—because Clara was still in school. It was decided that Meritable's home was a good meeting place, one in which Clara could flee to her room if necessary; she would not feel as cornered as she might at the hotel. Meritable left Etna with an embrace, which she returned. Though the circumstances had been difficult, Etna rejoiced in the fact that her daughter had been cared for by such a warm and sensible woman.

The five days until the meeting tested Etna's patience. Clara was so close and yet unreachable. What if Clara heard of the meeting and ran away before Etna could get to her? What if she refused the meeting and would not come out of her room on the appointed day?

Etna spent her time walking around Gainesville and the campus of the University of Florida to make the hours go faster. Even in early March, the sun was strong. She visited the town center, walked along University Avenue, and strolled along the streets of the nearby neighborhoods. She found the town center to be a small one: a grocery, a laundry, a photography studio, a pharmacy, and an ice cream shop. Most days, she retreated to her room and drew the shades. She had many memories to sort through, both distant and recent.

On Sunday, Etna walked to Meritable's house. As it was a hot day, Etna was perspiring and had nearly soaked her handkerchief from blotting her face and neck. She strode up the front walk, wanting to appear confident. Meritable, who had been watching for Etna, opened the door herself and led Etna into a sitting room that was deliberately kept dark to stave off the heat. Meritable reached over and opened a shutter so that they could see each other. After that, she left to fetch Clara.

Etna composed her expression into one of gentleness, for she did not want to frighten the child.

The door opened, and Clara stood before her. In an instant, four distinct emotions crossed the girl's face. Surprise at Etna's actual presence. A flash of joy. A sudden and fixed look of anger. And then, with chin raised, an effort to display a mask of indifference. Etna wanted to take her daughter into her arms. Perhaps she showed some astonishment as well. Clara had grown a good three inches in Etna's absence and had slimmed out in body and face. She wore a pair of trousers and a white sleeveless blouse, as though to say this was no special occasion for her. Her hair was lighter blond than Etna had ever seen it. Etna said, "Clara." And then, anguished, Etna watched as tears filled her daughter's eyes.

"Oh, Clara," Etna said again.

"I'm sorry," Clara blurted as she put an arm up to cover her face.

Etna went to her daughter. At first, Clara stood limp against her, but then Etna felt the faintest pressure against her back. She ran her hand through the silk of Clara's hair.

Etna drew the girl to the sofa and made her sit down. "It's I who am sorry," Etna said, receiving from Meritable a clean handkerchief to give to Clara. And in that simple gesture, Meritable made plain to Etna that she was the mother now.

Etna asked her daughter why she had apologized, and Clara said it was for lying to her mother about Phillip Asher. "I did it to bring you home," she added.

"And that is the best of all possible reasons," Etna said.

She did not belabor the point just then, knowing they would have time to talk later. She was, instead, struck by the wonder of having her child within her reach. She told Clara that it was she who had abandoned the family. Clara said she understood it was because Etna had been so unwell. Etna realized then that Meritable had left it to her to tell the truth.

She said, as gently as she could, that she had not been in a sanitarium, but had gone to France to serve as a nurse's aide in the war. Clara seemed bewildered by this news, and Etna knew it would take some time for her to absorb it. Etna added that Meritable had been told that Etna was ill and had never had reason to question that statement. Etna could see that the confession of her whereabouts altered Clara's imaginings of her mother and that their relationship had become more complicated, as it was bound to do. Imagining a mother sick in bed was one thing; knowing that she had been alive and well and at war was quite another. Of course, Etna had not been well, not well at all, but it might be weeks or months before Etna could explain that to her daughter.

"You're so beautiful," Etna said to Clara.

"How could you just go off to France and leave us?" Clara asked with sudden anger.

"The situation is complex," Etna began. "We will talk a great deal over the coming weeks. I think you have enough information now to overwhelm anyone. And there is really only one important fact you need to know: I love you very much. I always have and always will."

"I won't leave here," Clara announced.

"No one is asking you to leave. I'm not going to snatch you away, if that's what you are worried about. I'm staying at the hotel. You can visit me there. And I'll be coming to dinner here. If you are uncomfortable with this, you must say."

They did not touch again that afternoon.

\*　　\*　　\*

The days and weeks that followed were not easy for Etna, or for Clara. When Etna misread her daughter, the girl had sudden fits of anger that caused her to weep and once again ask the questions that could never be answered no matter how many times Etna attempted to. How could she tell the truth about Van Tassel and still have her daughter not think ill of him? Etna was not blameless, she had told the girl, but then she began to realize that Clara did not want her mother to be a guilty party. The child desperately needed one parent who would always say and do the right thing, who would be a rock in her shifting world, who would tell her how to behave, if necessary.

For the first time in almost two years, Clara had an opportunity to express herself on the entire matter. She was not yet in control of her feelings, however, and Etna determined that she herself must be steady and calm when they were together. That was all Clara wanted, a righting of the ship.

Several weeks after her first visit with Clara, and only after the two had established a solid bond upon which to build a new relationship, Etna made plans to visit Nicky.

Etna wrote to the headmaster of the Hackett School in Croydon, New Hampshire, and said that she would soon be coming to see her son and that she would send word from the hotel when she had arrived. She did not ask him to check with Mr. Van Tassel about the request, nor did she want Nicky to know about the impending visit until the day of the meeting itself. She explained her situation and where she had been and added that she hoped for good news of her son.

On the day of the visit, Nicky appeared in the headmaster's office and spoke at once. "You are my Aunt Etna. I have heard of you. You've come back from Europe to visit. I have a rule."

Etna was abashed to hear such abrupt statements issue from this small boy. She turned to the headmaster, who only shrugged.

"What is that?" Etna asked.

"You are not to speak of my mother."

"Why?" Etna queried, almost certain that her son knew that she was his mother. He had flinched slightly when he had entered the room and had colored with the same blush that used to bedevil his father.

"It is not allowed."

"Nicky."

"I am not Nicky. I am Nicodemus."

"This is the rule at your home?"

"No, it is the rule at all times. The staff here and at home have been informed."

My gosh, Etna thought. My son has turned into a little prig. The boy Etna used to tickle and hug and squeeze was suddenly a not-very-likable stranger to her. He even looked like Van Tassel, with his face and lips and heft, and he seemed to have used his father as a mirror for his expressions. Distaste, dismissal, and even, she thought as she stood there, a certain helplessness. Etna went along with "the rules" because she knew that Nicky would not leave the headmaster's office without her agreeing to them.

With their hats and coats on, they walked to the hotel across the street from the school. Nicky pointed out his room on the third floor of the building they had just left. Not with pride. It was merely fact. In the dining room, he snapped his napkin across his lap as he had seen his father do hundreds of times. For a while, they spoke of his studies, his friends, his interests. He favored dessert over lunch itself, and Etna indulged him. After a bowl of ice cream and a piece of chocolate cake, she asked him why they were not allowed to discuss his mother.

"She left me and my father and sent my sister to live far away."

"Did she?"

"Now I have no real family, which is why I am here."

Etna wanted to cover her face with her hands and weep, but knew she could not in front of her boy. "That must be very hard on you," she said.

"It was very bad at first, but now I have the hang of it."

"I'm glad," she said.

"There are boys here worse off than me."

"And how is that?" she asked.

"At least I have a father."

"So you do," Etna said. "Does he take you home on vacations?"

"Sometimes," Nicky said, looking away. "The big ones. Christmas and part of summer. Some of the boys have to go to other people's houses for *all* the vacations. I would hate that."

"Your mother did all this?"

His confidence faltered for just a minute, or perhaps he had an ache in his tummy from all the sweets he had eaten. "Yes, she did."

"Where is she now?"

"How should I know?" he asked. "You are her sister. You ought to know."

"Nicky," Etna said, for she felt it was time to stop the charade.

"Is it true that if you are in England you can hear the guns from France?"

"Yes," she said. "Sometimes."

Etna saw a tear forming at the corner of one eye. Nicky looked every bit the child he was. "I hardly knew her, you know," he said. "You look terribly like her."

"Nicky, you know who I am."

"You are my aunt!" he cried out in one last desperate attempt to shore up the fragile carapace around him.

"No, Nicky. I am your mother. Yes, I am Etna, but I'm your mother. I think you know this."

Nicky picked up his napkin and tied it around his eyes as though it were a blindfold.

"I have been to Florida and have visited Clara," Etna said. "She misses you, Nicky."

He shook his head. He was a curiosity in the dining room, and several women turned in their direction. Etna ignored them. "I love you, Nicky. Yes, it's true I went away. I felt I had a mission in Europe. Maybe I'll tell you about it one day."

Nicky drew the white cloth a half inch down his eyes. "You look an awful lot like her," he said.

"That is because I am her. I've only been away a little over a year. Even the dullest of boys wouldn't forget his mother in that time."

Her son waited, then seemed to collapse into the napkin, which had come undone. Etna reached across the table and held his hand. She waited for him to collect himself.

"I must go," he said, red-eyed, lowering the napkin. "I need to get back for class."

"We have plenty of time," Etna said, standing. They left the lobby and then the hotel.

"Where are you going after this?" he asked.

"I'm staying here at this hotel. I plan to see you often."

"I'm hardly ever free," he said.

"Nicky."

The boy dropped his head and gave his mother the quickest of embraces. He pulled away as if hoping no one had seen him do it. All Etna wanted was to hold him close to her.

As they drew nearer to the school, the Van Tassel in Nicky seemed to reassert itself. Etna hated to see it happen. It was clear to her that she had hard work ahead.

"I think we shall have to keep this a secret between us," he announced in the same voice he had used to issue his command about "the rules." "We shall say nothing to Father."

"If you say so," Etna said. "I love you very much. I will see you very soon."

"It will have to be on my schedule," he announced, and for a fleeting moment, she wondered if she had not lost him after all.

"What will you do when I am in school?" he asked.

"Do?" she asked as they reached the gate of the school. "Well, I shall draw. I'm an artist."

"Was Mother an artist?" he asked, narrowing his eyes.

"Well, I am your mother, and though I really didn't feel confident about being an artist in the past, I am one now."

"Can you do that?" he asked. "Just decide to become an artist?"

"Well, you could. It's better if you feel you have some talent."

"Are you any good?"

"I think so, yes."

"I play the piano," he said. "I started this year. I'm quite good."

"Are you?" Etna asked, suppressing a smile. She would start by taking her son as seriously as he took himself.

"I shouldn't go visiting my father if I were you," he warned.

"And why is that?"

"He has a terrible temper where my mother is concerned. He said she was gone for good."

"Well, I am not. But I won't go to see him if you'd rather I didn't."

Later, after Nicky had gone on to his class, Etna paid a visit to the headmaster. Mr. Price helped her to draw up a schedule during which she might see Nicky more often. Etna sensed in the man a sincere concern for the boy. He alluded to problems Nicky had had in adjusting to the school. Perhaps he felt that a mother's influence would help. Etna had no way of knowing whether the headmaster would contact Van Tassel. She knew that Nicky would say nothing.

Shortly after she had seen Nicky, Etna arranged for Clara to travel north to join them. Meritable and Etna had agreed that Clara, at sixteen, was old enough to make the solo voyage, and indeed, Etna's daughter seemed to be trembling with pride when she stepped off the train at White River Junction and embraced Etna. Clara wanted very much to see her brother.

After Clara had been fed, Etna collected Nicky at his school. When he came through the doors of the hotel and caught sight of Clara, who was waiting in the lobby, he ran forward and pushed his head into her stomach. This might have been taken for a hostile gesture, but Etna knew it had been his way of greeting his sister when he was younger. Clara batted him off, as an older sister must, yet Etna noted that she was grinning broadly when Nicky stepped back, his hair mussed and his face flushed. Etna had a waiter bring the pair of them cups of cocoa. After the children had settled into their warm drinks and had started to bicker as they used to do, Etna knew that all was well.

The three played in the snow until it was time for dinner. They ate at the hotel, in a dining room with a great fireplace. Nicky had become skilled at checkers, which pleased him enormously, since his skills enabled him to beat Clara for the first time. Later, when the three had settled into their separate beds in Etna's room, they remembered funny incidents from the past.

In the middle of the night, Etna was woken by an owl. The moon was up as she glanced at Clara. What she saw there moved her. Nicky had crawled into his sister's bed for comfort. They lay sprawled among the sheets, the covers thrown off. Clara had the pillow, and Nicky's head was more or less hanging over the bedside. The sight of her two children, in a bed right next to hers, was one Etna had never thought to witness again. She was both soothed and elated by the tableau. When she and Clara took Nicky back to his school, the three parted with a ferocious hug.

After her first several letters, Etna wrote to Dr. Bridge again. She had sent him a number of letters in the intervening months, keeping him abreast of her reunions with her children.

Dear August,

When I was in New Hampshire waiting for one of my visits with Nicky, I asked the innkeeper if I might borrow a motorcar. On the first day, I drove to Exeter, where I once lived with my family while my father taught mathematics at the boarding school there. Though every place one inhabits contains both good and bad memories, I tried to stay in a positive frame of mind. The preparatory school in Exeter has grown considerably since my father's time there, but it is slowly emptying as the students leave to join the war. Even juniors, I am told, are faking birth certificates. The school does not allow students to sign up—but really, what can they or their parents do? And I imagine that some parents are encouraging. (Well, the fathers, possibly. What mother has ever encouraged her son to war?)

My second excursion was not as pleasant, but it was one I felt compelled to make. I drove to Thrupp, meandered the streets of that grim college town, and saw the place where I once lived with my aunt and uncle. Finally, having found my courage while having a cup of tea at the Thrupp Hotel, I drove to the street on which I had lived with my husband and children. I wore a hat with a veil, and I knew that Van Tassel would not be expecting me. Nevertheless, it was with a great breath that I entered the street. The house has been meticulously kept up, but the garden is gone—razed completely. I felt no sadness or nostalgia and only a little fear lest Van Tassel open the door and call out to me, which did not happen. It is worth noting that I have not suffered from the specific ailment of a feeling of menace at the back of my neck since that day.

You are often in my thoughts.

Etna

*Counsel for the Relator wishes to address the court:*

"Your Honor," begins Mr. Hastings. "I have here a writ of habeas corpus for the body of a male child, Nicodemus Van Tassel, aged nine years, currently a resident at the Hackett School for Boys in Croydon, New Hampshire."

Etna blinks at the phrase *the body of a male child.* What a terrible thing, this legal language.

"He resides at the school?" Judge Warren Kornitzer asks.

"Yes, Your Honor, though technically he is in the custody of his father, Nicholas Van Tassel of Thrupp, New Hampshire, whom he sometimes visits during the school vacations."

"Mr. Bates," says the judge, addressing counsel for the Respondent. "Where is your client?"

Mr. Bates stands. "Your Honor, my client, *Dean* Nicholas Van Tassel, has judged his duties at Thrupp College to be of such importance that he cannot be called away for a matter he did not bring to the court."

"*Dean* Nicholas Van Tassel will appear in my court when he is ordered to," the judge says in a voice just this side of angry. "He should be ready to appear at any moment."

"I do request, Your Honor," Mr. Bates says, "that you give me fair notice of his summons due to the distance between his place of work in Thrupp and the court here in Newport. It would take the man the better part of two hours at least to get here if he were called. Four hours to get the message to him and back."

"The man does not own a telephone?"

"I shall determine if he does."

"You do that, Mr. Bates. Mr. Hastings, where is the child?"

"The child is at school, Your Honor. He can be produced whenever you think wise. It was thought that the child should attend to his lessons until such time as it is necessary for him to appear."

Judge Kornitzer searches through papers on his bench as though he has missed a fact or two.

"My client, Your Honor, is Mrs. Etna Van Tassel," explains Averill Hastings. "It is she who wishes custody of the young boy. As the court has already ruled, since Mr. Van Tassel will not grant Mrs. Van Tassel a divorce, the only means that Mrs. Van Tassel has to be with her son is to seek custody. My client's contention is that the boy has been forced into a boarding school at too young an age, and that even when he is not a resident at the school, his father often sends him away to camps and to other people's homes during the vacations. In short, the boy is not at all well supervised."

"And we know this how?"

"From the boy himself, sir."

Judge Kornitzer bends his head and closes his eyes. Etna has been told that the judge deeply dislikes cases in which young children must be brought in to testify.

"It is my understanding, Mr. Hastings, that the child has a sibling."

"Yes. Clara Van Tassel, currently living in Gainesville, Florida, with her aunt Meritable Root and her husband, Henry. Clara has lived with her aunt and uncle since August of 1915."

"And why is that?"

"This is owing to a great rift between the father and the child."

"What is the nature of this rift?" the judge asks.

"With your permission, Your Honor, that is a matter I wish to put more fully to the court at a later moment."

"And why was the mother, your client, not able to care for her own children all this time?"

"Your Honor, from early September, 1915, until October, 1916, my client served with distinction in the Voluntary Aid Detachment of the British Red Cross in Camiers, France, and with the Croix Rouge in Marne at great personal sacrifice to herself. She was unable to return to the United States until February, 1917."

Judge Kornitzer nods slowly. "What was her sacrifice?"

"She sustained injuries to her head and feet. She was forced to work under extreme hardship with constant fear of injury and death."

"Yet she chose this course of action, did she not?"

"She was under duress at the time she signed on."

"And what has your client been doing since February, 1917? If I am not mistaken, the date today is May 17, 1918. That is a year and three months. Where has she been?"

"She has been in this country spending as much time with her children as possible, and trying to make a decent living so that she may care for the boy."

"She does not want the girl?"

"Clara Van Tassel will turn eighteen this October. It is my understanding that Clara, as soon as she finishes her schooling in a few weeks' time, will come north to study at secretarial school in Boston."

Mr. Bates, Van Tassel's lawyer, snaps his head in Mr. Hastings's direction. This is news to him.

"Mrs. Van Tassel very much wants to be with her daughter and will be close enough that this will be possible," Mr. Hastings continues. "Clara, as I understand it, feels the same way. Therefore, there is no need to seek custody in her case."

"How is the mother getting her living?" the judge asks.

"She makes detailed drawings of surgical procedures at Mary Hitchcock Memorial Hospital in Hanover."

"How would she be able to care for a young boy if she must be at the hospital?"

"She visits the hospital once a week, makes sketches, and then goes home to perfect them. These drawings are said to be vital to the surgeons experimenting with new techniques."

"Very well, Mr. Hastings. We shall hear testimony in this matter." The judge sighs. "This is a complicated case, is it not?"

"Yes, Your Honor, it is."

"Mr. Bates," the judge says, addressing the lawyer sitting opposite Mr. Hastings. "What do you have to say for yourself?"

Mr. Bates, a fair-haired man in a light brown plaid suit, appears to be somewhat put off by the provocative tone of the judge. "I have a case, sir."

"Very well, state it."

"Your Honor, this is a simple matter," Bates begins, his face flushed, his gold-rimmed spectacles, in the light from the sole window, smeared. "There is no statute in the great state of New Hampshire that would prompt the court to give custody of a nine-year-old boy to the woman sitting to my left. Let us consider the facts. Etna Van Tassel fled her family house on August seventeenth of 1915 without so much as a good-bye to her husband or to her children. From that date until February of 1917—a period of a year and six months—they did not know where she had gone. There was no note, no letter from abroad, no person who came to the house with a message, no communication whatsoever. For all the children knew, their mother, whom they had loved deeply, had abandoned them forever or was dead. For that reason alone, Etna Van Tassel cannot be considered fit to be a parent, and I request that this case be dismissed."

Etna lightly scratches the back of her hand. Everything Mr. Bates has said is true. She has struggled to understand how it was that she did not write to her children. Hastings has told her she must think hard about her answer when he asks her this question on the witness stand.

"Hold on, there, Mr. Bates," says the judge. "As far as I know, this is not a simple case. Did I not just say as much? There may be good reasons why the case should be heard by the court. Or there may not. I cannot determine that at this time."

"But, Your Honor, even if the case were to be heard and mitigating reasons for Mrs. Van Tassel's absence found, which will not happen, how could the state ever trust the woman to be a steady parent again?"

"You make a good point, Mr. Bates. I hope to have the answer to that question during this hearing. Mr. Hastings, call your first witness."

*Counsel for the Relator calls Dr. John Hobson Gile to the stand.*

"Dr. Gile," says Mr. Hastings, "thank you for coming today. I know you are a busy man."

Dr. Gile nods. Etna is surprised to see her employer in New-port, the county seat, some twenty-five miles from Hanover.

"Dr. Gile, can you tell the court what you do for a living?"

"I am head of the surgical department of the Mary Hitchcock Memorial Hospital. I am also a professor of anatomy at the Dartmouth Medical School."

"You are acquainted with Etna Van Tassel, are you not?"

"Yes, I am."

"In what capacity?"

"I hired Mrs. Van Tassel to make detailed drawings of our surgical procedures while we are performing them. These are extremely valuable as teaching tools."

"Etna Van Tassel is in the operating theater with you?"

"Yes. It is quite unusual to find someone who has frequently witnessed surgical procedures and therefore will not flinch at the sight of open anatomy—and who is at the same time an expert draftsman. Draftswoman, I suppose I should say."

Mr. Hastings smiles. "And how would you describe her demeanor and her work?"

"She is dependable, easy to work with, and meticulous in her renderings. Her drawings are extraordinary, and, indeed, I intend to see that they are published in a book about surgical procedures."

"How did it come about that you hired her?" Mr. Hastings asks.

"She came to me, actually. She showed me a dozen drawings of doctors engaged in surgery at the hospital camps to which she was attached while she was serving in the war abroad. I was very taken with their precise execution and, to be frank, their beauty, even though the subject matter was—how shall I say...quite raw. I asked her if she had ever attended a surgical procedure, and she said she had done so dozens of times. I did not query her too much on her reasons for having left the country and served abroad. It was not unheard of at that time. I asked her to attend a surgery the following week and do a drawing for me, explaining that I would then decide if I could use her."

"And you were happy with the results of that trial?"

"Extremely."

"How long has she been in your employ?"

"Nearly a year now."

"If you do not mind my asking, how much does Mrs. Van Tassel earn per drawing? Or does she have a salary?"

"I recently offered her a salary of eight hundred dollars per annum for her services. I asked her to sign a contract, as I did not want to lose her."

Etna was relieved when he offered it to her. To have a contract of employment can only help her case.

"Have you ever had occasion to speak with Mrs. Van Tassel on matters other than surgery?"

"She works on Mondays, which is when we schedule many of the procedures for the week. She returns to my office on Friday afternoons to deliver her work. During those meetings, we have sometimes chatted, as colleagues will do."

Mr. Hastings, Etna can see, is visibly pleased with the word *colleagues.*

"Did she ever, during that time, mention her children to you?" the lawyer asks.

"Yes, she did. I believe we spoke about our families. I recall vividly her pride at telling me that her daughter, Clara, had been accepted at secretarial school in Boston."

"Did you talk of other matters?"

"I'm afraid I queried her at length about her time in the war. One rarely has a chance to speak with someone who has actually been in the hospital camps."

"Did she ever talk about her son?"

"Nicky? Yes, several times. Recently she mentioned that he was having a good time playing baseball at the Hackett School."

"Dr. Gile, would you recommend Etna Van Tassel to any of your colleagues at other hospitals?"

Dr. Gile bends forward as if to make his point better heard. "I would recommend Mrs. Van Tassel to any colleague anywhere, indeed to any employer anywhere. She has been a gift to Mary Hitchcock Memorial Hospital, and we hope she will remain with us for a long time."

"Thank you, Dr. Gile."

"Mr. Bates, do you have any questions for this witness?" asks the judge.

"Not at this time, Your Honor."

"Very well, Dr. Gile, you may step down."

*Counsel for the Relator calls Alice Beaumont to the stand.*

"Good morning, Mrs. Beaumont," Mr. Hastings says pleasantly.

"Good morning."

"You are Mrs. Van Tassel's landlady, are you not?"

"I have a house in Grantham. After my husband passed away fifteen months ago, I found the place too big for one person. And so I advertised for a woman of good deportment."

"That would be the woman you see behind me."

"Yes."

"What sort of tenant, if you don't mind my using the word, is Mrs. Van Tassel?"

"Well, the best sort, really. The rent is always on time, if that's what you mean."

"Does she ever mention her children to you, Mrs. Beaumont?"

"Mention them? I should say so. I have met them both."

"Objection," Mr. Bates says, standing. "Were these supervised visits?"

The judge addresses Mr. Hastings. "Were they supervised?"

"No, Your Honor, because there has never been any need for supervision. Both children visit willingly."

"Does Mr. Van Tassel know of these visits?"

"I cannot answer that question. Clara comes when she can, though the geographical distance between mother and daughter is very great. As for Nicky, I believe Mrs. Van Tassel makes arrangements with the headmaster of the Hackett School."

Etna remains completely still. She has been told by Mr. Hastings that by bringing the custody suit, she risks being banned from ever seeing Nicky again. Van Tassel can, and doubtless will, if he wins, forbid meetings between Etna and her son. At best, all she can hope for in that case would be supervised meetings. For a week after she was told this fact, Etna barely slept, going over the pros and cons endlessly as she sketched and drove and walked. She does not believe that Nicky should remain in boarding school any longer. He needs a mother's close supervision, and for that, she must have custody. On the other hand, if she had done nothing, she might have been able to continue seeing her son when he was free, as she has been doing.

The judge asks Mr. Bates if he has any questions, and again Mr. Bates says he does not.

"Very well," says the judge. "You may step down, Mrs. Beaumont."

*Counsel for the Relator asks to read aloud a letter from Captain Richardson of the Royal Army Medical Corps.*

"May I have a copy of this letter?" the judge asks.

"And I," Mr. Bates insists. "Your Honor, I object to the reading of letters from people not willing to show themselves in court."

"Mr. Hastings?" asks the judge.

"This is from a captain in the Royal Army Medical Corps who works as a surgeon at Camiers hospital number four in France, and I think even the court would agree that it would be impossible at this time to request Captain Richardson's presence in this hearing room."

"Objection overruled."

Mr. Hastings distributes copies of the letter. Etna is once again surprised by her lawyer's enterprise. Though she gave him the names of the institutions in which she had served, she did not know that Mr. Hastings had done such detective work.

"The date of the letter is April thirtieth, 1918. I shall begin.

"Dear Mr. Hastings,

"I was much surprised to receive your letter. The woman you wrote of was known to us as Etna Bliss. I am sorry to hear that she is involved in a custody dispute. I know firsthand that she wanted more than anything when she was with us at Camiers to return to her children. I recall specifically a morning quite early in her stay with us when she came to me asking to be dismissed from her position so that she could return to America to see them. I must say I did not take kindly to this request. I pointed out to her that she had signed a contract for one year of service in return for her training, and that all of us had children we would dearly love to see again. I was, I think now, a bit harsh with her. But the point was that we simply could not spare her.

"I will not distress you with a description of life in hospital camps in France, but I can tell you that Etna Bliss was a most valuable asset to our work, ready to step in at a moment's notice when needed. In those months, it was not uncommon for personnel to be asked to undertake tasks they had little training for. In Miss Bliss's case, I recall asking her if it was true she could drive a large car (she had written this on her original application), and when she said yes, I asked her to drive an ambulance for us, since driver attrition at that time was dreadful. I think I may have told her that. If I did, I am now doubly impressed by how ready and willing she was to take on this role. There was an occasion in January of 1916 when she demonstrated exceptional bravery by leaving the designated route back to camp with an ambulance full of wounded during an unexpected bombardment. I regret that I did not on that occasion applaud her actions publicly, though if you have gotten to know the woman at all well, you will understand that she would not have wanted that sort of attention.

"We were surprised and alarmed when it became clear

that she was no longer with us in March of 1916. I was thus happy to hear from one Dr. August Bridge that Etna Bliss was now well and living in America.

"I should like to express at this time the gratitude of an entire nation to the United States for its considerable contribution to our war effort.

"I wish Etna Bliss and you well in this legal matter, and I hope for a swift and happy conclusion.

"Yours sincerely,

"Captain Angus Richardson"


*Counsel for the Relator asks to read a letter from Sister Luke of the Sisters of Our Lady Convent, Abyssinia, Africa.*

"Mr. Hastings, you may proceed," says the judge.

"The letter is dated April tenth, 1918.


"Dear Mr. Hastings,

"Yes, I do remember Stella Bain quite well. As she must have told you, she was, when she arrived at our hospital camp, injured in her feet and in her head, and she had as well lost her memory. She called herself Stella Bain, but I understood the name to be a made-up one, since she certainly did not know who she was. She had, by the way, been left at our door during the night of March 14, 1916, by a man hauling a cart with her in it. She was unconscious for three days before she woke in our tent.

"Once she recovered from her injuries, I found Stella Bain to be an industrious nurse's aide, even though her French was poor. She was a quick learner and shortly absorbed the necessary hospital French to do her duties. A quiet woman, hardly talkative, she was older than most of the nursing sisters there. She asked, or rather begged, to drive an ambulance, and after an initial trial, proved adept at that task as well. I hope she has told you that we did not see her again after a scheduled leave to Paris. We had no word of her for some time. I understand now that she was under severe mental distress during her time in both Marne and London, for I had a letter from a Dr. August Bridge letting me know that she had returned to America. It was then that I learned her true name, Etna Bliss Van Tassel. I was astonished to discover that she had gone back to see her children. I had not known she had children in America, and I am not sure that she did, either.

"I should not like to see Mrs. Van Tassel come to any further harm. I would give her the highest reference to any employers who might want them.

"Yours in Christ,

"Sister Luke"

The men in the courtroom observe an unasked-for moment of silence, as if in respect for the Catholic sister toiling in Africa.

*Counsel for the Relator calls Etna Van Tassel to the stand.*

"Mrs. Van Tassel, how are you this morning?"

"I am well, thank you."

"Can you tell the court why you are in this hearing room today?"

"Yes, I can. I wish to gain custody of my son, Nicodemus Van Tassel. Mr. Hastings, may I refer to him as Nicky during these proceedings?"

"Your Honor?" Mr. Hastings asks.

"Yes, very well."

Etna is aware of the judge's intense scrutiny, as though she were of a slightly different species. He displays his thoughts and emotions via black bushy eyebrows that have marvelous flexibility.

"You are currently living at One seventeen High Street in Grantham, New Hampshire?" Mr. Hastings asks.

"Yes, I am."

"Why have you chosen that address?"

"It is close to Croydon, where Nicky is at school. And it is not too far from Mary Hitchcock Memorial Hospital, where I work."

"How do you get to work?"

"I drive a car, a Ford T."

"Is it true that you drove a Red Cross ambulance during the war abroad?"

"Yes, it is."

"Were you ever under bombardment while acting as a VAD?"

"Yes, I was."

"Were you ever under bombardment while serving as an ambulance driver?"

"Yes, I was."

"Can you tell the assembled why you went to France?"

Etna takes a long breath. Of all the questions Hastings is likely to ask her, this is by far the most difficult. It is also the most crucial. "This will be a long answer, Mr. Hastings."

"Proceed."

"In the early summer of 1915, my husband and I had grown apart. I was living with our daughter, Clara, then fourteen, in a cottage I had purchased in Drury, New Hampshire. Nicky, then six, was living with his father. In order to bring Clara and me back to the house, my husband convinced our daughter, Clara, to tell an outrageous lie. She said that my husband's rival for the post of dean of Thrupp College, a Mr. Phillip Asher, a man I had known when he was a boy and more recently as an acquaintance, had touched her inappropriately."

"Did you believe your daughter?"

"At first, no. I could not believe that Phillip Asher, who seemed to have an unblemished character, would do such a thing. But then my daughter made a gesture that was so appalling, so personal, that I thought her incapable of making this up. I was horrified, but I was compelled to accept my daughter's accusation. She was a child. I didn't even know she knew such things were possible. That she should demonstrate the gesture seemed damning in itself."

"So you returned to your husband's home."

"Yes, I did. I felt that Clara needed both parents to support her."

"And then what happened?"

"My husband sent a letter to the chief of police in Thrupp and to the board of corporators at Thrupp College with the charge. Phillip Asher, who had won the post of dean, was immediately fired by the college and interrogated by the police. He left Thrupp in disgrace, his academic reputation destroyed. Later in the summer, my husband told me that Phillip Asher had gone to

France as a pacifist and was serving as an ambulance driver with the British Red Cross."

"How did you feel when your husband told you this?"

"I was deeply shaken. I felt that we had sent a man to his likely death. I was afraid my daughter would not forgive herself for having spoken up about this matter, and yet I believed she had done the right thing in bringing the matter to our attention. Mostly, I felt ill in both body and soul."

"Then what happened?"

"Shortly after her father said that Phillip Asher was in France, Clara called out to her father and asked if she *could tell now.* My husband tried to hush her, but I was instantly alert to something amiss. I pressed my daughter as to what she meant and learned that what she had said about Phillip Asher was a lie. She had been coached by her father to tell this lie so that I, her mother, would return to the family home, which I had done, and also so that Mr. Phillip Asher's reputation would be ruined."

"This was on August seventeenth, 1915."

"Yes."

"What did you do?"

"I was enraged. I went up to the guest room. I needed time to think. I tried to write to Phillip Asher, but I could find no words to convey my deep apology for what my family had done to him. I hated my husband then and would not admit him to the guest room, where I was staying."

"And what about your daughter, Clara?"

"I knew that Abigail, our housekeeper, would keep an eye on both Clara and Nicky, who was too young to understand what was going on. It was my intention to go to Clara in the morning and talk about the incident with her. But I knew I needed to calm down first."

"And then what happened?"

"It was a stifling night. It had been humid and hot for weeks, and I had the window open and the door ajar to get any kind of a breeze that might be blowing. I had fallen asleep without thinking to lock the door. At some point, I do not know precisely when, my husband entered the room. He had been drinking."

Etna is silent. She cannot tell this next part. Not to the men assembled in the room. It feels prurient and disgusting. She tries to gather herself together.

"Mrs. Van Tassel, I know this is difficult for you," her lawyer says encouragingly.

"Watching a man die is difficult for me, Mr. Hastings. I can answer your question. My husband assaulted me. He tore my clothes and hurt me."

"Would it be fair to say that he raped you?"

"Yes, it would."

"Objection." Mr. Bates rises, nearly spitting. Perhaps he has been wanting to spit during Etna's entire testimony. "Your Honor, no husband can be prosecuted for rape in this state."

"Your Honor," Mr. Hastings counters. "We have no intention of trying to prosecute Nicholas Van Tassel at this time. This testimony is intended to reveal why my client felt she needed to flee the house."

"The testimony will be allowed," the judge says.

"Mrs. Van Tassel, can you tell us what happened after the assault?"

"I felt that if I did not run from the house, my husband would kill me. The situation he had created was intolerable. I waited until he had fallen asleep, and then I ran. Well, not literally. I took my motorcar and drove away."

"And where did you go?"

"I drove to White River Junction, where I caught the first train to Boston. I was afraid my husband would follow me. At the same time, I believed it was urgently necessary to find Mr. Asher in France and make amends to him for what our family had done to him. I know this doesn't sound logical now, but I was not in my right mind. I believe no woman is after she has been raped."

"Objection," says Mr. Bates, rising. "Mrs. Van Tassel is in no position to know how all women feel after they have been assaulted, if that is indeed what happened. I further object to such crude language being used in this court."

"Mr. Bates, this is a hearing room, and a fact is a fact, crude or not. Please sit down."

"Mrs. Van Tassel," asks Mr. Hastings, "can you continue with your answer?"

"When I arrived in Boston, I saw a poster at the train station advertising the need for young women to sign up for passage on a Red Cross hospital ship. Under the auspices of Massachusetts General Hospital and Harvard Medical School, it was scheduled to cross the Atlantic to tend to the wounded in France. Training for nurse's aides would take place aboard ship, at Southampton, and in France. As it happened, the training stopped the very second we set foot on French soil. The true nursing began then."

"Mrs. Van Tassel, at what point would you say that you regained your wits?"

"That is a hard question to answer, since it was difficult to keep whatever wits one had to begin with under those terrible conditions. But I believe it must have been around October of 1915, as Captain Richardson suggested in his letter."

"To reiterate, you asked to have your contract broken so that you could return to your children."

"Yes, I did."

"Objection," shouts Mr. Bates. "Your Honor, is it necessary to have this testimony repeated? I believe we all understood it when it was read out."

"Objection sustained. Mr. Hastings, would you please move on to your next question?"

Mr. Bates sits with a satisfied expression on his face. A point to him.

"What happened to you in regard to your desire to return to your children after that?"

"Common sense told me I could not just slip away from the camp and go AWOL. I might make it as far as a hospital ship going to the coast of England or even to London, but then what would I do? I did not have the means to travel back to America and would not have until I had fulfilled at least a year of my contract."

"And that was it?"

"Yes, until I spoke with Phillip Asher. He suggested I look up his brother, Samuel Asher, whom I had once known in Exeter, at the Admiralty in London. Phillip thought his brother could help me."

"And how did you find Phillip Asher?"

"He found me. He had heard I was looking for him." Etna squeezes the fingers of her right hand. "A few months later, after a bombardment, he was terribly wounded in the face. He was brought into our hospital camp," she says in a quiet voice. "His face was shattered."

"What happened when you saw Mr. Asher's face?"

"There are no words, Mr. Hastings, to express how I felt."

"I am sure there are not."

"I tried to comfort him and to follow him into surgery. I was certain that he would die. I was prevented from remaining near the surgical tent. I ran out of the tent and fell to my knees. Then I ran into a field. That is all I remember."

Hastings moves to the other side of Etna. "You remember nothing about what happened to you after you ran into the field?"

"I did not remember anything about Phillip Asher until I recovered my memory, nearly ten months later."

"But you do now remember what happened to you during that memory loss."

"Yes, I do. I woke in a hospital tent in Marne. I will never know, I suspect, what happened between the time I ran into the field in Camiers and woke up on the canvas cot in Marne. I was very confused. I remember trying to guess at a name and coming up with Stella Bain. I called myself Stella and was known as Stella Bain all the time I was in Marne. I believe now that the name came to me because it is more or less an anagram of Etna Bliss."

"At some point, you left France with the intention of going to London."

"Yes. I had heard a soldier mention the word *Admiralty* when I was working in Marne. Immediately I began to obsess about the word. I thought if I could find out what *Admiralty* meant, the mystery of my memory loss would be explained."

"And was it solved in that place?"

"Yes, but not until many months later."

"Mrs. Van Tassel, during the time of your memory loss, did you know that you had children?"

"No, I did not."

"You were abroad from September of 1915 until early March of 1916, a time of six months, during which you could not leave France to get back to see your children."

"That is correct."

"And from early March of 1916 to January of 1917, you did not know you had children."

"Yes, that is correct."

"And what happened when you finally realized who you were and that you were a mother to Clara and Nicky?"

"I was stunned. Shamed. Worried. Before the week was out, I was able, through the generosity of Captain Samuel Asher, to obtain passage on a merchant ship leaving London for Cuba. I took another ship to Jacksonville, Florida, and a train to Gainesville, where I was shortly reunited with my daughter, Clara."

Mr. Hastings turns away from Etna and addresses the judge. "Your Honor, may I request a recess? I do not want to exhaust my client, and I see that we have gone beyond the lunch hour."

The judge contemplates Etna. "Yes," he says. "We shall adjourn until ten o'clock tomorrow morning. Mr. Bates, I think this would be an opportune time for you to convey to your client the earnestness of the court's request that he appear in this hearing room tomorrow."

"Yes, Your Honor."

"Thank you, Mrs. Van Tassel," the judge says. "You may step down now."

"Court dismissed," the bailiff calls out.

The next morning, when Etna sees Van Tassel moving toward her from the end of the corridor, she stands as still as an animal wishing to remain invisible. He is deep in conversation with Mr. Bates, who seems to be trying to persuade his client about something—a conversation Etna cannot hear. Van Tassel has aged, but so has she. More so than he, she suspects, because of her time in France. Her husband (she can barely think the word) has grown older in a way one might have expected: his body is rounder, his hair has begun to thin. He has a triple chin, which she does not remember from before. He seems, as he moves closer to her, to be a self-satisfied member of the gentry rather than a scholar: a man who eats well and entertains a great deal, a man who owns horses and land.

When he catches sight of Etna, Van Tassel stops while his hapless lawyer keeps on walking. Van Tassel's blue eyes widen and his face is suffused with the blush that is more than a blush; he looks apoplectic. She waits for the color to slowly leach from his face. As he grows colder and his eyes narrow, he walks toward her.

"Etna," he says with feeling, and for an awful moment, Etna thinks he will embrace her. "How *dare* you do this to me?"

Etna cannot pretend that he does not terrify her. The last time she saw this man was on a bed after he had raped her. But now she is at least capable of standing her ground. "I am not doing this *to you,* as you put it," she says in a quiet voice. "I simply want to be a mother to my children."

"You forfeited that right years ago."

Etna can see a yellow stain on her husband's shirt. He has perspired all the way through to his suit coat.

"The court will decide that," she says.

"You are no mother," Van Tassel declares, lifting his chin. "You are a whore and a harlot."

"I believe the latter two are one and the same. In any case, I am neither."

"I have evidence that you went straight to Samuel Asher's home in London when you arrived there. That you lived with him in sin."

Mr. Bates has a hand on Van Tassel's elbow. "Dean Van Tassel, you are above this. You are wanted in court."

"Who gave you that evidence?" Etna asks her husband.

"A detective I hired."

Etna smiles. "You were misinformed."

Van Tassel points a finger at Etna even as Mr. Bates is trying to drag his client away from the encounter. "You will be sorry for this."

Etna holds her hands tightly in front of her. "I sincerely hope not," she says.


*Counsel for the Respondent calls Dr. George Church to the stand.*

"Good morning, Doctor."

"Good morning."

"Can you tell us where you work and what your specialty is?"

"I work at the Mary Hitchcock Memorial Hospital, and my specialty is psychiatric illness."

"Have you ever had occasion to witness memory loss in a patient?"

"The condition is extremely rare. I have seen it only in cases of serious blows to the head. The memory loss is almost always short-lived, perhaps two or three days in duration. I have seen a similar condition in patients who appear to have sustained memory loss, yet when subjected to scrutiny confess that they only wish they had."

"Is it your opinion that a woman who may or may not have sustained an injurious blow to the head could have lost her memory for ten months?"

"I do not believe that is possible. I would be more inclined to diagnose that woman as suffering from hysteria that appeared to present as memory loss."

"Would the patient know that the memory loss was false?"

"From time to time, yes, but such would be her hysteria that she would be able to convince herself that her memory loss was real."

"Thank you, Dr. Church."


*Counsel for the Relator wishes to cross-examine Dr. Church.*

"Good morning, Dr. Church. I have just two questions."

"Yes."

"Have you ever met, let alone examined, Mrs. Van Tassel?"

"No, I have not."

"Have you ever treated patients coming directly from the front in Europe?"

"I have not had an opportunity to do so. No."

"Thank you, Dr. Church. That is all."

*Counsel for the Respondent recalls Mrs. Van Tassel to the stand.*

Mr. Bates stands eagerly, carrying a sheaf of notes toward Etna. How many questions can be in those papers? she wonders.

"Mrs. Van Tassel, how are you this fine morning?"

"I am well."

"I am glad to hear that. You have told the court that you were married for fifteen years."

"Yes."

"During that time, did you purchase a house in Drury, New Hampshire? Specifically, on February ninth, 1914?"

Etna dares not glance at Mr. Hastings. He knows about the cottage, but he has chosen not to bring up this potentially damaging fact. Etna thought her lawyer wrong in this and said so. She has lost her advantage now. She has lost the ability to tell the undistorted truth.

"I did."

"Can you tell the court why you purchased this house?"

"It was not a house. It was a one-room cottage. I purchased it so that I could have a place to read and draw and sew and write."

"Simple pursuits, you would say."

"Yes."

"And you could not do those things at home?"

"I could do them," Etna says, trying to explain the impossible. "But it wouldn't have been the same."

"And why is that?" Mr. Bates queries.

"I felt I needed to have a place of my own. A place where I could breathe."

Mr. Hastings, at his desk, drops his head. Wrong answer.

"You did not feel you could breathe in your own home?"

"Of course I could," Etna says, trying to stay for a moment longer above the fray. "It's an expression. It means I needed a place where I might find solace."

"Again, I would ask," says Mr. Bates, somewhat more dramatically, "why you could not find *solace* within the bosom of your family? With your *children?*"

"I believe every man or woman is entitled to a space where he or she can think without the demands of one's relationships."

"But you were a mother, Mrs. Van Tassel. Indeed, that is why you are in a courtroom today. Do you think it proper for a woman to have a life apart from her duties as a mother?"

Etna hesitates. This will go hard on her. "Not a whole life, but a small portion of that life, particularly if it will not harm anyone else."

"Indeed," says Mr. Bates, making no secret of his disapproval. "Did you tell your husband about this house?"

Mr. Bates uses the word *house* deliberately.

"I did not."

"And why was that?"

"It would no longer have been mine."

"Objection," says Mr. Hastings, rising. "I should like to remind the court at this time of the Married Women's Property Act, which has made it legal for women to hold property of their own."

The judge scrutinizes the lawyer. "I do not think that was an objection to Mr. Bates's question. Objection overruled."

Mr. Hastings sits, but he has made his point and reminded the court of Etna's legal right to own a cottage.

"Mrs. Van Tassel, if you discovered that your husband had bought a house for his own purposes and did not tell you about it, how would you feel?"

"Objection!" says Mr. Hastings, again on his feet. "Mrs. Van Tassel cannot be required to answer a hypothetical question."

"Objection sustained."

"Very well. Mrs. Van Tassel, did your husband discover that you had this house?"

"Yes, he did. He followed me there one day."

"And how did he respond?"

"He was very angry."

"I can imagine. Most men would be. He must have thought you had been having an affair."

"Objection!" This from Mr. Hastings.

"Sustained. Mr. Bates, please do not speculate."

"Yes, Your Honor."

Etna replies nonetheless. "I most assuredly was *not* having an affair. As for my husband, I cannot say for certain what he thought. He was not himself. He destroyed things in the room. He said he would divorce me."

"Did you believe him?"

"I did not know what to believe. It seemed inconsistent with what I knew about him."

"In any case, you took the children and went to live with your sister, Miriam, in Exeter."

"Yes."

"Why is that?"

"Our marriage was broken. I was afraid of my husband. In addition to discovering the cottage, he did not receive the post of dean. It was a time of many disappointments, and he was reacting in a volatile way."

"Were you visited in Exeter by a Mr. Tucker, Esquire?"

"Yes, I was."

"And why did this man drive all the way to Exeter?"

"He came to take Nicky back to his father."

"And did he explain why?"

"Yes, he did. He said that a woman who had purchased a cottage for immoral purposes was seen to be immoral. Any woman seen to be immoral was considered by the state to be a bad influence on her son, and thus the son could be removed from her care. Mr. Tucker did not seem to want to hear that there had been no immoral purposes in the first place. I might add that Mr. Tucker was not concerned about Clara, who was also with me. The state, apparently, does not care about daughters."

"Mrs. Van Tassel, let us not get carried away," says Mr. Bates.

"I do not believe I am carried away," says Etna. "The purpose of Mr. Tucker's visit was nefarious. He had been encouraged to visit Exeter and take Nicky away from me by my husband, whose goal was to have his wife return to Thrupp. He knew that I would not let Nicky live too far from me."

"Did Dean Van Tassel ever confide that to you?"

"No, he did not."

"Then you cannot know what was in his mind. Perhaps he simply wanted to follow the law in this matter."

"I can tell you this, Mr. Bates," Etna says, even as she glances at her husband. "The last thing Mr. Van Tassel would have wanted was to have me leave his home. He was, and I hope the court will forgive me for saying such a bold thing, obsessed with me. Did he love me? Yes, I suppose he did. In his way. It is difficult to tell where love ends and obsession begins. In his case, I think it was the other way around."

"Your Honor," says Mr. Bates. "Would you please instruct the witness to answer the questions I put to her simply and plainly, without embellishment?"

The judge knits his eyebrows together. It is some time before he delivers his opinion on the matter. "Mr. Bates, I have always been of two minds on this issue. On the one hand, I like proceedings to move along swiftly in this courtroom. But not at the expense of the truth. In my experience, I have often found that the second statement from the witness often contains more truth than does the first. I shall not at this moment rein in Mrs. Van Tassel's answers, but I will not hesitate to do so if they are not immediately pertinent to the question at hand."

Mr. Bates seems to take unfavorable judgments quite hard. When he asks his next question, he has already transferred his anger to Etna.

"*Mrs.* Van Tassel, is it true that Nicky went to live with his father, and that you went to live with Clara at the cottage?"

"Yes."

"Did Mr. Phillip Asher, your husband's rival for the post of dean of Thrupp College, ever visit you there?"

"Yes."

"Did he ever visit you when Clara was present?"

"Yes, he did."

"Did you not think his visits in *questionable* taste, if not out-right *immoral?*"

"No, I did not. He came to the cottage as a friend only."

"But it *was* possible for someone to imagine that Mr. Asher had made advances toward you and possibly toward your daughter?"

"One can imagine anything, Mr. Bates. But the truth is the truth, wouldn't you say?"

"I am not required to say anything, Mrs. Van Tassel. In early August of 1915, what caused you to return to your husband's household?"

"He said that Clara had something of importance to tell me."

"How could your husband know that Clara had something to tell you if she was living with you exclusively?"

"She and her father sometimes had dinner out together."

"I see. And the important thing was?"

"Objection!" shouts Mr. Hastings. "The witness has already spoken of this matter quite fully. The court does not need her to do it again."

"Objection sustained. Move on, Mr. Bates."

"Mrs. Van Tassel, during your fourteen years of motherhood, did you ever take your children to church?"

Etna is taken aback by the abrupt transition. "I did."

"Every Sunday?"

"No, not every Sunday."

"How many times a month would you say you took your children to church or Sunday school?"

She has had time to prepare her answer. Why then is it so hard to respond? "I took the children to church and Sunday school at least once a month."

Mr. Bates looks astonished, aghast. Etna hopes he is not as good a lawyer as he is an actor. "Were they given religious instruction at home?"

"No, they were not. My faith was not strong at that time."

"I see. And now?"

"My faith is nonexistent as a result of having seen so much death and destruction during the time I spent in France."

"And speaking of that, Mrs. Van Tassel, can you explain to the court why you did not tell your children or your husband where you were from the moment you left the house in August of 1915 and your return to this country in February of 1917? It is my understanding that they had no letter from you, no telegram, no transatlantic call, no message from you through a relative, no form of communication at all."

How clever of Mr. Bates to make it seem as if Etna has brought the question upon herself. The query has been asked casually, but its intent is anything but casual. It is at the heart of Mr. Bates's case: how can a mother abandon her children and then expect them to be returned to her when she wants them? But Etna's *answer* is at the heart of Mr. Hastings's case. She must not only respond to the question but also do so in such a way that it does not damn her forever.

Etna raises her head and forces her hands to remain still in her lap. "When I left the house, I was afraid for my life. I was not afraid for my children's lives. I knew that Abigail would protect them, and I did not believe Mr. Van Tassel would harm them. He was obsessed with me, not them. The desire to flee from him merged with the desire to make amends to Mr. Phillip Asher so powerfully that I was temporarily deprived of rational thought.

I also hoped that Mr. Asher would forgive Clara, for she was in a terrible state at the time. Once I boarded the hospital ship in Boston, I could not return, and the court already knows why I could not. As for writing to them, I believed that Mr. Van Tassel would not pass along the letters to my children but rather would read them himself. He might even be tempted to distort what I had written to persuade my children that I was never coming back."

Van Tassel makes a sound and squints at her.

"I had a second reason, not as important as the first," Etna continues. "Though I doubt Mr. Van Tassel would have had the means or the wherewithal to snatch me back from France, I did not want him to know where I was. Once I had made the decision to go AWOL from the Royal Army Medical Corps and seek advice from Samuel Asher in London, I felt I could better explain everything to my children in person and without their father's intervention. But as we know, I did not make it to London until eight months later, and when I did, I did not know I had children."

This is her answer. It will have to stand.

*Counsel for the Respondent calls Dean Nicholas Van Tassel to the stand.*

"Good morning, Dean Van Tassel," Mr. Bates begins in a cheery voice.

"Good morning." Van Tassel doesn't exactly sniff, but his bearing suggests he thinks the proceedings and even the judge beneath him. Etna can only imagine what he might have to say about Mr. Bates, his own lawyer.

"During your fifteen years of marriage, did you love your wife?" asks Mr. Bates.

"I loved my wife. Yes, I certainly did." He says this as if in the faculty club, ordering cod for dinner.

"And from your point of view, how do you account for her absence after the night of August seventeenth, 1915?"

"After she left the house and did not return for some time, I hired an investigator to discover where she was. I personally thought she had gone to London. I told the man so and paid for him to travel there and report back. I thought she might be living with a Mr. Samuel Asher, brother to the aforementioned Phillip Asher."

"And what did the investigator report to you?"

"It was as I expected. He reported that my wife was living with a Mr. Samuel Asher in London."

"Were you shocked by this information?"

192 • Anita Shreve

"I was hurt, but not shocked."

"And why is that?"

"I had come across some letters my wife had written in which she spoke of a love affair she once had with Mr. Samuel Asher. I thought she had gone off to be with him."

"How would you characterize Mrs. Van Tassel's demeanor during the marriage?"

"She was cold."

"Was she a good mother to your children?"

"I suppose so. I was often away. Abigail, our housekeeper, spent the most time with our children."

Etna wants to stand and shout, *Untrue!* Mr. Hastings, beside her, puts a restraining hand on her arm.

"Dean Van Tassel, you have a position of considerable importance at Thrupp College, do you not?"

"Yes. You yourself have just addressed me as Dean."

"You must have many duties."

"I do."

"Has this left you time to be with your son?"

"As much time as any father with serious responsibilities has. Nicodemus is in school for most of the year, so I can rarely see him then, except for Parents' Day and so forth. I try to have him all the other days of the year, although he is a popular boy and is often invited to stay with his friends. Since I think it of the utmost importance that he should fit in at the school and make good friends, I often agree to these invitations."

The sour expression on Mr. Bates's face indicates that he is sorry he has asked that question. Perhaps he would like to get his client off the stand as soon as possible.

"Dean Van Tassel, do you think your wife a fit mother for your son?"

"I can hardly call her wife. I have not seen her in three years. Before today, I am not sure I could have described her. No, she is not a fit mother at all. She abandoned both of her children needlessly. She broke their hearts." He pauses, and his face threatens to lose its composure. "May I also say that she broke mine."

Etna knows this to be a true statement.

"I have no further questions for this witness," says Mr. Bates.

"May I return to my duties at school?" Van Tassel asks the judge.

"No, sir, I am afraid you cannot. Be patient a while longer, if you would. Mr. Hastings, do you have any questions for this witness?"

"I do."

"Very well, proceed."

Mr. Hastings stands, adjusts his suit coat, and approaches the witness box. He is all business. "Dean Van Tassel, did you in the summer of 1915 ask your daughter, Clara, to lie?"

"Objection! We have been over this material."

"Your Honor," argues Mr. Hastings, "I think it important that we hear the story from Dean Van Tassel's point of view."

"Objection overruled."

"Dean Van Tassel," says Mr. Hastings, "you may answer the question now."

"Not precisely, no," Van Tassel says. "She may have misinterpreted something I said. Children do that all the time."

"We are speaking of the matter of Mr. Phillip Asher having touched your daughter inappropriately."

"Of course we are."

"When Clara made the inappropriate gesture referred to earlier in these court proceedings, you knew it was not true."

"It may have been true. How was I to know?"

"As I understand it, Clara admitted the lie later in the summer. She said you had asked her to lie."

"Children are often fanciful, Mr. Hastings."

"If we had Clara here, what would she say about the matter?"

"Objection!" says Mr. Bates, rising to his feet. "You are asking the witness to speculate."

"Objection sustained."

"Dean Van Tassel, how long has it been since you have seen your daughter?"

Etna scrutinizes her husband. He has been evasive, but he cannot sidestep this question.

"I have not seen her since September of 1915."

"And why is that?"

Van Tassel swallows. Etna can see the color rising in his neck. "After my wife abandoned us, I consulted with my sister, Meritable Root, who lives in Gainesville, Florida. We corresponded. Clara seemed beside herself with grief for her mother, who had abandoned her. My daughter would not speak with me about the matter, which did not surprise me. A daughter always wants her mother at that age, does she not? It was decided that Clara would stay for a time with Meritable and her family until such time as Meritable deemed Clara fit to return."

"But that has not happened, Mr. Van Tassel, has it?"

"No, and I fault my sister on this matter."

"Do you? During this time, did you write to your daughter or receive letters from her?"

Van Tassel turns his head away from the lawyer. Etna remembers Van Tassel's love for Clara when she was young. The way they used to take walks together, the girl's hand so tiny in his. Such ruination, such destruction. And all Etna had to do so long ago was to say no to Van Tassel's proposal in the parlor of her sister's home.

"No," Van Tassel answers finally. He sits up straight and adjusts his vest.

"Did you, in the summer of 1915, write and send two letters describing Clara's charge of impropriety on Mr. Phillip Asher's part? These would have been to the chief of police in Thrupp, and to the president of the college?"

"I may have done."

"Did you understand the seriousness of those accusations?"

"Of course I did. I did not, nor have I ever, acted dishonorably."

Etna is struck by Van Tassel's pronouncement. She is certain that he practiced it before his appearance in court. She wonders if he actually believes it.

"Mr. Van Tassel," Mr. Hastings continues, "can you tell the court the number of days your son has lived with you this past year?"

"Of course not. No parent counts the days a child is with him."

I do, Etna thinks.

"Have you ever been to the Hackett School, at which your son is enrolled?"

"Of course. I settled him in."

"And when was that?"

"Two and a half years ago now."

"Who takes him to school and back on vacations and holidays?"

"Well, due to my heavy schedule, it is often not convenient for me to ferry him back and forth, and so I leave that to our housekeeper, Abigail, who can now drive a motorcar."

"Can you tell the court what sports your son plays at school?"

"I do not believe he is old enough to play sports."

"Can you tell me what your son's interests are?"

"His schoolwork takes all his time. He has none left over. I imagine his interests are the normal ones for boys."

"Your Honor, that is all at this time."

"Dean Van Tassel, you may sit down," says Judge Kornitzer. "But your presence is required in the courtroom."

"Really? Must I stay? I have said my piece."

"You will remain in this room until court is adjourned. There may be additional questions for you later."

*Counsel for the Relator calls Headmaster Edward Price to the stand.*

"Good day, Mr. Price."

"Good day."

"You are headmaster of the Hackett School for Boys."

"Yes."

"How long have you held this post?"

"Eleven years."

"Mr. Price, you understood when Nicodemus was first brought to the school that he had one guardian only?"

"It was not precisely stated. But neither Mr. Van Tassel nor his son mentioned a wife or a mother. When I finally questioned Nicky, he said, 'She has gone away and left us.'"

"When Mrs. Van Tassel did appear in your office in February of 1917, did you not think to call Mr. Van Tassel and inform him of the woman's presence?"

"Not at first. I simply thought she had come back from wherever she had been. I did note that she was staying at the hotel across from the school, but that is not at all uncommon for the parents of our boys. Nicodemus, I remember, seemed very pompous when he saw his mother for the first time. He referred to her as his aunt, which alarmed me, but when I was looking out the window for their return after the noon hour, I saw Nicky give his mother a quick hug. Later, I began to wonder why Mrs. Van Tassel always stayed at the hotel and why her husband was never with her. I queried her on this at her next visit. She said she was estranged from her husband, and that she did not inform him of her visits. I felt that my obligation was to the parent paying the bills, and so I called Dean Van Tassel twice, once at the college and once at home. I left a message with his secretary at the college and a message with his housekeeper at the house. Mr. Van Tassel returned neither of those telephone calls. I felt that I had discharged my duty, and I confess I was reluctant to see any harm befall the relationship between Nicky and his mother. I could see the good it was doing the boy."

"You did not attempt to reach Mr. Van Tassel at a later date?"

"No, I did not."

"I have no further questions."

"Mr. Price, you may step down," Judge Kornitzer says. "Thank you for your testimony here today."

"You're welcome."

\*　　\*　　\*

*Counsel for the Relator calls Edward Ferald to the stand.*

Instantly, Etna feels a charge, like one that precedes an electric storm. Ferald is a man her husband used to hate.

Perfectly tailored and coiffed, Ferald seems not to have aged at all. Well, why should he seem older? It has been only three years since she last saw him. That in itself seems an astonishing fact. Has it been only three years? It is a lifetime and more to Etna.

"Mr. Ferald, can you tell the court how it is that you know Dean Van Tassel?"

"The man was once my professor. He failed me in his course. Later, after quite a successful career, I attained a position as head of the board of corporators of Thrupp College, and I knew Mr. Van Tassel in a different way then."

"Can you be more specific?" asks Mr. Hastings.

"We had recently lost a beloved dean of the college, and it was up to the board to select from among several candidates the one best suited to step into Noah Fitch's shoes. Mr. Van Tassel was a candidate. I did not think much of the man—and not simply because he had once failed me; I rather think I had risen above that—but because he seemed weak. Not only in his scholarship, which I had reason to believe fraudulent, but also in his ability to be a leader."

"When you say that Mr. Van Tassel's scholarship was fraudulent, what do you mean?"

Van Tassel stands. Etna thinks he is about to open his mouth and lodge a protest against this witness. Perhaps he plans to. To everyone's surprise, however, he simply turns and leaves the room. When Etna glances at Ferald in the witness box, he has a small smile on his face. Has he, once again, triumphed over his old rival?

"Mr. Bates, is your client taking a personal break?" asks Judge Kornitzer.

"No, Your Honor. I am sorry to say that my client just announced to me his intention to leave the courtroom and return to his duties at Thrupp College."

"Did you tell him he would be held in contempt of court for such an action?"

"I did not have a chance to, Your Honor."

"Mr. Bates, you do not seem to have any control over your client."

"I am sure he will return."

"Are you? He will pay a hefty fine for that walkout. Mr. Hastings, I am sorry for this interruption caused by Mr. Bates's client. You may proceed."

Ferald can barely contain his pleasure.

"Mr. Ferald, I had just asked you to explain what you meant when you said the words 'fraudulent scholarship' in relation to Mr. Van Tassel."

"As I was researching Mr. Van Tassel during my deliberations as to his candidacy, I came across a notation of a meeting between the previous dean and Mr. Van Tassel. It was a matter of plagiarism. I will not bore the court with the details of the case, but I did call Mr. Van Tassel into my office to discuss it."

"How did he react?"

"He was upset. He denied the charge, even though Dean Fitch had made clear notes on the matter. I think the fact that Mr. Van Tassel immediately dropped his candidacy for the post after our meeting speaks for itself."

"Mr. Ferald, we do not allow things to speak for themselves in court," says Mr. Hastings. "Did you think Mr. Van Tassel guilty of plagiarism?"

"Yes, I did."

"Is this a crime the college takes seriously?"

"Oh, I should say so. For a professor, there is no greater crime."

"Why have charges not been brought against the man?"

"At the time, I felt that the resignation of his candidacy was enough punishment. As I no longer am associated with the college, I cannot bring the charge myself. I imagine the notes are still there, if Mr. Van Tassel has not destroyed them."

"Objection!" This from Mr. Bates. "The witness may not speculate on Mr. Van Tassel's behavior."

"Sustained."

Mr. Hastings turns toward the judge. "Your Honor, I request a small break at this time. Yesterday I received correspondence that I believe will have bearing on these proceedings, and I wish to study the letter more thoroughly. I have brought copies of this letter and will give them to both the court and to Mr. Bates should I decide to use it. And I see that we are once again nearing the noon hour."

The judge checks the clock on the wall. "The court will recess for one and a half hours so that we may eat," he says. "Court will be in session at two o'clock."

"What letter?" Etna asks when her lawyer returns to her.

"I'll tell you later. I suggest you try and eat something."

*T*he Honorable Judge Kornitzer calls Mrs. Van Tassel to the stand.

"Mrs. Van Tassel," begins the judge. "Did you enjoy your lunch?"

"I did. Thank you, Your Honor."

"Well, I much enjoyed mine. I have several short questions I should like to ask, as they have been bothering me as we near the end of this hearing."

"Yes, sir."

"How and where would you and your boy live if you were to gain custody of the child?"

"We would live at One seventeen High Street in Grantham."

"Where you now reside."

"Yes. We would live as mother and son. Mother and son and daughter, when Clara can be with us."

"Will you be removing the boy from the Hackett School for Boys?"

"Yes, I will. I will be entering him in the primary school in Grantham."

"A public school," muses the judge. "With a lesser reputation."

Etna squares her shoulders. "That depends upon one's point of view. Though I have tremendous respect for Headmaster Price, I believe Nicky should be schooled in a more democratic environment and be allowed to form friendships in the neighborhood where he lives."

"Don't you think it might be upsetting for the boy to be removed from the only school he has known?"

"It might be at first, but I doubt it. He has great need of family right now, of a mother specifically."

"What if you are not satisfied with the quality of the education he is receiving at the primary school?"

"I shall supplement his education where I feel there are gaps. I did that for his sister, Clara, when she was younger."

Judge Kornitzer nods. "The court is sorry you were not here when your son needed you most."

Etna, chastened, answers. "I am, too, Your Honor."

"Mrs. Van Tassel, although I do not allow hypothetical questions in my court from counsel, I am going to put one to you now. If you were in my position, with this decision to make, would you allow a mother who had once abandoned her children to have custody of them again?"

Etna must say yes, she must. But the question, in its phrasing, is damning and makes her hesitate when she should not. There is no time. "Yes, Your Honor. I would give custody of that boy to his mother because she loves him with all her heart."

"You may step down, Mrs. Van Tassel. Thank you."

Etna, shaking, returns to her position beside Mr. Hastings. He gives her a long quizzical look to ascertain if she is well. She nods.

*Counsel for the Relator wishes to read aloud a letter from Dr. August Bridge, surgeon, of Bryanston Square, London.*

"Is this the letter you spoke of earlier today?" the judge asks. "Do I and Mr. Bates have copies of said letter?"

"Yes, it is, and yes, you do."

"Very well, you may read it into the record."


"Dear Mr. Hastings,

"I was very glad to have news of Etna Bliss Van Tassel, but saddened to learn that she is now involved in a custody dispute over her son. I have the utmost admiration for Mrs. Van Tassel, and I hope the courts will see fit to allow the woman to be mother to her child. She certainly has earned the right.

"I knew Mrs. Van Tassel as Stella Bain. This was not a pseudonym or an alias, but rather a name that came to her when she woke from unconsciousness in Marne, France, in March of 1916. In late October of 1916, the woman made her way, against great odds, to London, because she believed something at the Admiralty in London to be the key to retrieving her memory. She arrived, in a destitute state after her long journey, at the square in which my wife and I lived. We took her in, as anyone would an indigent. Because I was a cranial surgeon with a growing interest in psychological matters, Mrs. Van Tassel and I quickly discerned that my help might be useful to her. She had lost her memory, she said, and wanted it back.

"She became a guest in our household as well as a quasi-patient of mine.

"It is my opinion, based on what I observed during her stay and the study I have pursued since, that Mrs. Van Tassel was suffering from shell shock when she came to us."

Etna flinches at the diagnosis. Though she thought it might be true when she met with Dr. Bridge in the orangery, neither he nor she ever said the words.

"Though I was at first reluctant to compare Mrs. Van Tassel to those whose minds have been shattered in the trenches, I have reached the conclusion that she suffered from a like illness.

"To my knowledge, Mrs. Van Tassel may be the first diagnosed case of female shell shock in my country. I have no doubt that there are other women with this condition who have not come forward. Logically, it must be possible. Nursing sisters and their aides abroad see nightmarish injuries and death all around them. Worse, they not only see the injuries repeatedly, they must touch them in the most unpleasant ways, and then watch most of the men die. These women must be plagued by the same physical and emotional symptoms as male soldiers.

"Although Mrs. Van Tassel's shell shock took the form of memory loss, which my colleagues in this country are discovering is not an uncommon symptom in men who have returned from the front, Mrs. Van Tassel also suffered from intermittent seizures, a deafness that came upon her from time to time, and severe, not to say ghastly, pains in her legs, which rendered her incapable of moving for five minutes or so. To my knowledge, Mrs. Van Tassel no longer suffers from seizures or deafness, and I am quite sure that after all this time, the pains in her legs have gone away.

"Mrs. Van Tassel worked tremendously hard while under

our roof to unlock her memory. She did this, with my help, by way of talk therapy, therapeutic drawing, and a strong hunch on her part that led to the place where she finally heard her true name spoken aloud by Captain Samuel Asher of the Royal Navy. He was a man who had known her when she lived in America. At the moment she heard her true name, she recovered her memory.

"The very first words Mrs. Van Tassel spoke when she realized who she was were *I have children.*

"I believe a subconscious urgency to be reunited with her children led her, under desperate circumstances, from France to London to the Admiralty. It is my understanding from Captain Asher that Mrs. Van Tassel was able to leave London almost immediately after regaining her memory and travel by ship to America. I have had several letters from Mrs. Van Tassel since that time and have learned that she and her children have been reunited.

"In England, we struggle to understand shell-shocked victims. At the beginning of the war, such men were accused of malingering and sent straight back to the very arena they were incapable of enduring. Today, we have hospitals set up for these men, where they receive various forms of treatment. Memory loss is not an uncommon symptom of shell shock; indeed, these hospitals report memory loss for up to two years and possibly longer, since the men they refer to have not yet recovered their memories.

"It is my private belief that Mrs. Van Tassel's shell shock was brought on not by a physical injury to the brain but rather by a previous trauma in America that was exacerbated

206 • Anita Shreve

by the trauma of her wartime activities and then sharply
crystallized by the sight of Phillip Asher's horrific wounds
to his face. Mrs. Van Tassel lost her autobiographical memory at that moment, or shortly thereafter. And that was a
rather good thing for her. I have no doubt that had she not
lost her memory, she would have had an irreversible breakdown in her mental health. As far as I can tell, there is no
known case of memory loss reappearing in a shell-shocked
victim. In other words, there is little to no likelihood of
Mrs. Van Tassel's losing her memory again.

"Mrs. Van Tassel is a woman of exceptionally strong character, stamina, and determination. She is graceful in her
bearing and in her interactions with others. In addition,
I believe she has a great capacity for love. I should think
any child of this woman would consider himself among the
luckiest persons on earth.

"Please give Mrs. Van Tassel my regards. I wish you both
a speedy conclusion to what must be for her a painful pro-
ceeding.

"Very sincerely yours,

"Dr. August Bridge"


A hush extends over the court. Even Mr. Bates is, for the moment, silenced. The solemnity and horror of the war has, perhaps
for the first time, entered the chill courtroom.

Etna weeps quietly for the war's victims, for August, for mothers who must see their boys off to war, and for herself. Mr.
Hastings, beside her, covers her hand with his own. Although

August has written with the best of intentions, and perhaps with great affection for her, he has unwittingly provided the one piece of information that will sink her case. The average person in America, Etna guesses, knows little about shell shock except that it is a terrifying diagnosis.

Judge Kornitzer gathers himself together and speaks into the silence.

"Court is adjourned until tomorrow morning, after which time I shall deliver my opinion in this case. Mr. Bates, make sure your client is present in the courtroom."

*The Honorable Judge Warren Kornitzer requests silence in the court-room.*

"Mrs. Van Tassel, I will direct my comments to you, since it is you and your lawyer who have brought the case to the attention of this court. You do not have to stand.

"I am convinced of your many excellent qualities. Your steadiness, your reliability, your good effect on your child, your ability to be an able mother, and your excellent character. In addition, I personally would like to thank you for your extraordinary service during this war, even though it took place before America entered the hostilities. Compassionate service to any soldier of any country is among the highest ideals of mankind. At the very least, your example must have given your British counterparts a good impression of an American volunteer.

"But being a good mother entails more than being of good character.

"I am minorly concerned that you left your children with no explanation as to how or where they could find you. I say *minorly* because I have no doubt that you would never, under any circumstances, do that again.

"I am disturbed that you would remove your boy from the only school he has ever known—one that is superior, moreover, to the one you would have him enter.

"I am very worried that you might not take your children to church. Society, and by that I mean the general body of citizens in this state, believes that regardless of the private beliefs of either the mother or the father, it is the parent's sacred duty to provide religious instruction for the child.

"Mrs. Van Tassel, the information this court received yesterday as to your diagnosis of shell shock and the physical health matters that attended it are deeply troublesome. The state cannot release a young child into the care of a mother who might, for any amount of time, become physically incapacitated.

"If you wish to pursue this matter further, I am going to require you to undergo a course of therapy for six months, after which I will request your appearance in this court with affidavits of your complete cure from a physician recommended by the court. At that point, if you wish, we will continue with our proceedings. No parent or relative of Nicodemus Van Tassel may remove the child from the state at any time for any purpose. I will bring charges of kidnapping against any person accused of doing so. When we reconvene, I shall expect both Nicodemus and Clara Van Tassel to be present in the courthouse.

"Note, Mrs. Van Tassel, that I am not forbidding you to see your son in the manner in which you have been doing, nor can the father forbid you to do so.

"The court wishes you well in your treatments.

"Court is dismissed."

Etna lies atop her quilt, staring at the ceiling. Supine is the only position she can manage. Never has she felt so exhausted, defeated, unable to stand. Once again, she is amazed at the power of the mind over the body. Just a few words spoken in court have rendered her as helpless as she was after three days traveling from France to London under impossible conditions.

Averill Hastings apologized as he walked Etna to her motorcar, Etna upright, determined not to show any weakness while others might be watching.

"Mrs. Van Tassel, I thought Dr. Bridge's very powerful recommendation of you to the court outweighed any comments about your previous illness, which he seemed convinced was cured," her lawyer said. "I did not expect that his use of the term *shell shock* would go so hard on you. I was wrong, and I cannot tell you how deeply sorry I am. But I still have hope. In six short months, you will have done as the court has asked and will be reunited with your son forever."

"Mr. Hastings, you are very young."


Just as Etna was about to enter her motorcar, a large figure appeared beside her.

"Etna."

She turned to look at the man who was once her husband. "Nicholas."

"I am sorry you had such a difficult experience in Europe."

Etna was astonished. And yet she remembered that empathetic face.

"And I am also sorry for the misunderstanding that made you flee my house."

*Misunderstanding.*

*My house.*

"Nicholas, it was no misunderstanding."

His eyes instantly filled with tears. She had seen this before, too.

Van Tassel sniffed the tears away. He did something with his chin that altered his appearance and closed a door that had, for a few seconds, been left open.

"Indeed. I shall pretend that this never happened," he said and turned. She watched her husband, who was no husband, walk away.


Dr. Bridge, the unwitting source of her demise. She understands his letter in a way the judge did not. In England, people are encouraged to get on with life: a son has died, a man has shell shock, do your best. But here, where the war is only a year and a half old, the words *shell shock* must seem both foreign and terrifying. She worries about the judge's recommendations. How will she find a physician in New Hampshire who will understand the nature of the diagnosis?

She hopes Dr. Gile can help her in this matter. A teaching hospital might have physicians who have studied the phenomenon. Or he will advise her to visit a military base. But what military doctor would have time to treat a woman?

She lies with her arms loosely at her sides, her feet slightly apart, as vulnerable as she has ever felt. A new thought enters her mind. She will have to tell Clara of her ailments; they are public knowledge now. Etna has no doubt that her daughter will love her just the same, but might the young woman begin to worry, to believe she must now be parent to the parent?

August... if only Etna could go to him, work with him again, and have him write a letter definitively stating that she is cured of all possible manifestations of shell shock. But then again Judge Kornitzer might not accept August's letter. He seems to want an independent, American physician to pronounce her well.

"Nicky," she says aloud, sitting up. She must go to see the boy today. Mr. Price will still be in his office, and possibly he will allow Etna, given the circumstances, to see her son for just an hour after classes. A glass of root beer in the hotel dining room will help Etna enormously, and it might, with any luck, lift Nicky's spirits, too.

6 June 1918

Dear Etna,

I have just received Mr. Averill Hastings's letter of 25 May informing me of the unhappy judgment rendered by the court in your custody case. Although he did not say it in so many words, I gather that his decision to read my letter out loud was the very thing that did you in. Since it was my *intention* that the letter be read out on your behalf, I have only myself to blame. Such a stupid, foolish, and unforgivable thing I have done to you! I thought that a clear statement of what you had been through and what you had overcome would weigh heavily in your favor. I should have realized that a diagnosis of shell shock would disturb the judge.

Etna, forgive me. No, don't forgive me. I don't deserve it.

August

June 30, 1918

Dear August,

I am allowed to see my children as before. Clara, as you may know, has come north prior to starting secretarial school in Boston. It is tremendously healing to know that both children are now within my geographical grasp.

August, I do not forgive you for the letter because there is nothing to forgive. I understood it as intended. Though I might blame my young lawyer for not better imagining the consequences of the letter, I can in no way blame you. In fact, I am grateful to you for trying to help me, as you always have done.

Etna

July 5, 1918

Dearest Phillip,

I hope that you are well. I have written several letters to you with no reply. It is not that I have expected a reply; it is just that I would like to hear from you. I wish for your good health in every way.

Your brother, in his brief notes to me, informs me from time to time of your progress. I understand that you are now living in Kent in a rather grand house with lovely grounds—an estate that is a rehabilitation hospital for men with your sort of injury. I was happy to learn that, because I would not like to think of you in a London hospital just now.

I am still living in New Hampshire and am in the process of seeking custody of my son, Nicky. I have had a minor set-back, and will have to try again in six months' time.

I found a thing of beauty the day before yesterday. I traveled to the seashore with Nicky for an outing. We stood on a rocky promontory and watched the navy blue water crash against the rocks of an island not far from shore. As we stood there, a red motorboat crossed the white spume of the waves. I imagined the vessel making its way to you.

Fondly,

Etna

As Etna contemplates the view outside her doctor's office near the top of Beacon Hill in Boston, she winces at the lack of progress she and Dr. Ambrose Little have made. It took six sessions to explain all that happened to her abroad and another six to talk at length about her mother and father, whom she has not seen since their deaths in the late 1800s. The greatest insight to emerge from those sessions was that Etna seems to have patterned herself after her teacher-father, not her cold mother, leaving Etna in a woman's body with womanly desires but an emotional state of mind that mimics that of a man: she is exceptionally rigorous in her draftsmanship, wants to learn more about medicine, and, most important, has spent most of her life desiring independence.

None of this does Etna *know* to be true, since Dr. Little seldom speaks during her time with him. He will neither confirm nor deny her insights, a practice that invariably makes her more anxious when she leaves his office than when she walked in the door. Sometimes, in his oak-paneled room with the two large floor-to-ceiling windows overlooking Mount Vernon Street, Etna feels adrift, not sure when to speak or what to say. She has written to Mr. Hastings twice to request another therapist, but Mr. Hastings has reassured her that a clean bill of health from Dr. Little is as good as a win in her custody battle.

She understands Dr. Little to be engaging in Freudian therapy. He has insisted that Etna lie upon a chaise while he sits slightly out of sight. She is glad for that, since he has a peculiar aspect and a porcupine beard. The quills stick out evenly and have been cut in the round.

The office is old, heavy with must. If she were to blow upon the tops of the many books on the shelves, she would produce billows of ancient matter. Someone routinely runs a carpet sweeper over the Turkish rug, but no one has recently swept under the tables or in the corners. She doubts that Dr. Little even notices. His universe seems to consist of the immediate environs of his desk and chair; it barely incorporates the chaise upon which she reclines. She wonders if he is married. Cannot be. That porcupine beard!

Etna sees the psychoanalyst only once a week because the train to Boston takes four hours. She spends the night in a hotel not far from Clara's school, and the two often have supper together after Etna's appointments.

Etna has discussed the war, the battles and the tents, her memory loss, and her symptoms with her therapist. She has at length gone over her marriage, her children, her time with Dr. Bridge, her love affair with Samuel, her friendship with Phillip. Dr. Little almost never breaks the silence.

Today she has been talking about her time as Stella Bain. It is material she has already covered at least twice, but she has run out of new topics. The pains in her legs are still a mystery to her. They seem a thing apart, an affliction that will be with her always. Perversely, they have only grown worse and more frequent. Before Mr. Hastings read the words of August's letter, Etna would have said she had the pains every six weeks or so. She had even gone as long as two months without them. But now they seem to come more and more often—three weeks between episodes—increasing the likelihood that she will experience them at a highly inopportune moment: while driving, for example, or while walking with Nicky, or at dinner with Clara, or while sketching a surgical procedure. Etna believes that only her extreme willpower has kept such scenarios from occurring.

Next week, just before Christmas, she will have finished her six months with Dr. Little. Six weeks ago, as she was nearing the end of the six months, she had to lie to him: she said that she thought the pains in her legs had finally left her. That day, she told him that she has inklings before an attack that the pains will come upon her, and that she had not had any such inklings in months. Periodically, since that time, she has mentioned the lack of pain in her legs, being careful not to touch upon the fact that if Dr. Little pronounces her cured, she can go back to the courts and try again for custody. When she does, she will insist that she has had a change of heart about religion and will take Nicky to church every Sunday. She will do her best to persuade the judge that the health and well-being of a child are perhaps more important than the name over the front door of the school he attends. Mr. Hastings, to whom she has also had to lie (about the pains), has been encouraging about her chances in court after the new year.

But privately, Etna is concerned. She worries that the increased frequency of her ailment has something to do with the fact that she is about to end her care with the therapist. She is tired of the pain and frightened of the very possibility the judge alluded to: becoming incapacitated in a dangerous situation. If she had stayed with August, would the pains have gone away by now? Of course, to have remained in London would have meant all this time without her children, which is now unthinkable. They have given her so much joy.

Sometimes Etna wonders if Dr. Little even understands what shell shock is. Or has he all along thought her merely another woman with a case of hysteria? In the beginning of the treatment, he handed her a packet of pills that she knew were for sleeping. What good were sleeping pills to her? She needs insight and clarity. When he asked her at the beginning of the following session if she had taken the pills, she told him no. He seemed neither pleased nor displeased.

"I have thought a great deal about how Stella and I are alike and how we are different," Etna says.

"Mrs. Van Tassel, our session is now over."

Etna is always surprised by the abrupt ending of the sessions. It seems unnecessarily rude. She swings her legs over the chaise and sits up. She reaches for her coat and hat and handbag and stares at the older physician. He is taking notes. Maddeningly, he will not look up at her, and he will not say good-bye.

She cannot imagine Dr. Little pronouncing her cured next week. What will he do? Write a letter to the judge? Surely he will not make any pronouncements to her.

There is one other gambit she might try, a ploy she has been thinking about all week. It will cost her another month before she can be a mother to Nicky, but it is time to end this charade for good.

\*    \*    \*

Because it is snowing heavily, Etna holds on to the wrought-iron railing as she descends the steps of the brick mansion. Has psychology bought the house for Dr. Little, or did he inherit it from his family? She cannot imagine him with a family. She has paid a hefty fee for her sessions, though Dr. Gile and the court have helped to subsidize her treatments, which, as far as Etna is concerned, have been no treatment at all.

When she reaches the bottom step, she has a sudden and clear picture of what the town of Boston looked like just a month earlier, when the Armistice was declared. Such joy, such incomparable joy! She went immediately to Clara's school and asked if her daughter might be allowed to have a late lunch with her mother. Together, they joined the throngs in the streets and ate a meal at a hotel that had a view of the Public Garden, filled with men and women and children giving thanks, in various ways, for the end to the horror to which so many Americans lost their lives. As she sat at the table with Clara, Etna imagined the intense relief in London after four devastating years of war.

Now, at the top of Beacon Hill, Etna thinks it might just be possible to catch a nearly empty troopship returning to England to pick up the thousands of American men and women still trying to get home. Etna will explain to Nicky and to Clara, both of whom will be at school while she is away, what it is she intends to do. Nicky, teasing, will ask if she will be his "aunt" again, but mostly he will be disappointed that the war is over and that he cannot go with her.

She will have to persuade Judge Kornitzer of the worthiness of her plan, and to do that she must have August refer her, in writing, to Dr. Richard Parkhurst, his colleague and a world-renowned specialist on shell shock, whom he has mentioned to her in their correspondence. August will need to persuade Judge Kornitzer that a British psychologist is more qualified than an American physician to work with her, since British physicians have seen so much more of shell shock than Americans have.

What she will not tell the judge is that it is Phillip she must see.

*London, January 1919*

A glistening white frost, greenish-brown where footprints have been. Etna has come for a walk in the garden on this Saturday morning, only her second day in London, to gather courage before knocking on August's front door. He is expecting her.

Even the pollarded plane trees glisten in the pale light, and it occurs to Etna that she has never seen them in leaf. She has missed two springs since she was last here, and she will not see the spring of 1919, either. On the docks and in the train stations of England, she encountered troops still returning from wherever they had been—Abyssinia, Russia, the Dardanelles—a vivid reminder of all the soldiers who have not yet been demobilized. Above the reception desk at her hotel stands a discreet sign reminding guests that ration cards still need to be produced. The women in the streets look emaciated, and there are so many more of them than there are men.

Etna spends a pleasant fifteen minutes meandering around the garden with its myriad footpaths, even though she is cold inside her wool coat and leather boots. She would like a fur—what woman would not?—but she is unlikely to purchase such a luxury. She must pay back Dr. Gile the money he has lent her for the treatments and the passage to England; she must save for Clara's tuition for next year; and she must begin to see to Mr. Hastings's bill. It could be years, if ever, before she has the money for a fur, and by then she will have other, more important, expenses to see to.

When she can, Etna notices precise shades of color. She has begun to experiment with color in her drawings; she's purchased thick, porous paper and uses the watercolor paints given to her by the Bridges. She does not want to paint like a watercolorist, using water liberally and painting quickly with pale tints. For her work, she needs saturated colors. Just finding the correct shade of red for blood took her days of trial and error. The particular shade of blue-purple for viscera was even more difficult. Though the task is time-consuming, it involves all her senses and leaves her in a blissfully trancelike state.

Before she left New Hampshire, she and Dr. Gile spoke at length about her proposed trip to England. He consulted with Mr. Hastings, and together they made a request of Judge Kornitzer: would he be able to meet with Mrs. Van Tassel about a matter of importance? The judge replied that he would, but that he wished both children to be present as well. Since the meeting was to take place during the week after Christmas, it would be easy for Clara and Nicky to attend.

They met in the judge's chambers in the courthouse.

"This young gentleman must be Nicodemus," the judge said as he rounded his wooden desk to take a seat behind it.

"Yes," Etna said. "And this is my daughter, Clara."

"I'm very pleased to meet you," the judge said, studying the young woman in the gray plaid suit. Nicky, who wore his school uniform, sat up straighter.

"Well, young man, do you hate the Hackett School as much as I did when I was a boy?" the judge asked Nicky.

Nicky colored but answered, "No, sir," without much hesitation.

The judge smiled. "Do you both understand that your mother intends to go away to England to find a doctor who will help her get better?"

"Yes, Your Honor," Clara responded.

The judge nodded. "You do not need to address me so formally in here," he said gently to Clara. "Here I am simply Mr. Kornitzer."

"Yes, sir," she said, turning to look at her mother.

"And you understand the length of time she will be away."

"One month," Nicky said. Observing her son, Etna thought that no back had ever been straighter against a chair.

"Well, I think we will have to give her six weeks. She must get there and back. Mrs. Van Tassel, you do understand that you may not leave before the children have returned to their separate schools and that you must show Mr. Hastings here that you have a return ticket?"

"Yes, I do."

The judge leaned back in his leather chair and took in Etna and her children. "You are quite an unusual family," he said and paused. "But not an altogether impossible one."

As she rounds a corner, mulling over that conversation, Etna sees the man she has not set eyes upon since early February of 1917.

"Etna."

Once, she heard her name spoken and it brought back her memory. Today, it brings a strong desire to embrace the man in front of her on the path, and she does so.

He holds her for a long time. She has missed his scent: laundry starch and soap.

Awkwardly, they break apart. She studies his face. He is clean-shaven, and his hair has been cut shorter, but the navy eyes behind the silver spectacles are precisely as she has recalled them.

"August," she says for the first time.

"I thought you might be out here," he replies. "You, like me, would have arrived early, I reasoned. And I was right. Are you cold?"

"No, no, I'm fine." She feels as though she knows this man well, and yet really she knows nothing of his life since she last saw him. Except for one fact.

"I am so sorry about Lily."

He nods. "She was too young."

"And how is the boy?"

"He's a handful," August says with a smile. "A joy, really. You shall see him in a minute. Let's head toward the house. Streeter is eager to greet you again."

Iris would have been let go, Stella thinks, since there was no longer a mistress to care for.

August holds out his elbow, and Etna takes his arm. She remembers that his stride is longer than hers. Silently, they compromise so that they can easily walk together.

Streeter, who must have been waiting at the door for them, opens it before they have mounted the first step. The man does not smile, never smiles because of his bad teeth, but she can see his welcome in his eyes. He bows. "Mrs. Van Tassel," he says.

"I should very much like to be Etna. You'll forgive me, but I am an American, after all."

"I am happy to see you again," Streeter says.

"And I you," Etna answers.

"Streeter, bring us tea, if you would," says Dr. Bridge. "And then fetch Sebastian. I know Etna would like to meet him."

Etna follows August into the morning room, not much changed since she saw it last: the same red tiles of the fireplace surround; the tulip chandelier. She sits on the red silk settee and recalls vividly the first time she entered the room, she in her filthy VAD uniform, Lily in her rose-colored suit.

"I'm remembering Lily," Etna says when August has taken a chair across from Etna.

"It was a difficult birth, a brutal birth," he says. "We found out shortly after you left that she had a condition called placenta previa. Perhaps you know of it?"

"With my Latin, I can guess. The placenta blocks the birth canal?"

"Precisely. She had to be put to bed. Knowing Lily, you can imagine how she chafed at this prohibition. I tried to amuse her in any way I could, and I almost always took my meals in her room. At the moment of crisis, I was sleeping in a spare room close to hers. Because of Lily's condition, the plan was to take the baby by cesarean two weeks before her labor was due to begin. Indeed, she was to be moved to hospital that morning. We had hired a midwife who lived in, but she slept upstairs. I was the first to hear Lily moaning. It was already nine o'clock, and I never oversleep. I see that fact as just one more part of God's diabolical plan."

He pauses. Etna wants to cover his hand, but he is too far away.

"By the time I got to the room, it was nearly over. Lily had

gone into labor a half hour earlier. When the placenta finally rup-
tured, she died within minutes."

"Oh, August. How awful." Etna briefly closes her eyes. "How
did you save the child?"

"I grabbed a knife and performed the cesarean myself. I had to
do this while she was still alive, though unconscious. It was..."
He shakes his head, as if to throw off the memory.

"Oh, my dear."

"It was what she wanted," he says. "I had to do it. I saw no
purpose in losing both of them."

As if to buttress the necessary deeds of that morning, a young
woman arrives with a toddler in tow at the same time Streeter
comes in with the tea.

August stands. "Etna, may I introduce Lucille, our nanny, and
my son, Sebastian Cornelius Bridge."

"Such a long name for such a little boy," Etna says, standing
and bending to the child. She smiles. He has Lily's blond hair,
but that is all of Lily Etna can see in him. "I am from America,"
she says. "Do you know where America is?"

Sebastian nods, pauses, and then shakes his head. "I have a
little boy, too," she adds. "Well, *you* might think he was a big
boy."

The child runs to his father, who swoops him up and holds him
over his head, then gently sets him down. "Well, I'm not going
to be able to do *that* much longer. You're growing too big," he
says to his son and takes him on his lap. The nanny stands at a
distance.

"Has he had his lunch?" August asks.

"Not yet," Lucille says.

"Oh, too bad, I was going to spoil him with one of these scones."

"Oh, I think he would not mind a scone, sir."

Etna thinks how unlucky and lucky this household has been. The boy is a treasure, a gift. She has never seen August so comfortable in his surroundings.

"You look criminally healthy," August says when they are alone.

"I have been too well fed."

"Nonsense. Your time in America has allowed you to become the woman you were meant to be. How are your children?"

Etna takes a long breath and lets it out. "It hasn't been easy, August. I've had to fight hard for our current arrangements, which, as you know, are not perfect." Etna removes from her handbag two photographs, both professionally posed. In one, a young woman with the shape of Etna's face and her mouth gazes at the viewer, a slight smile on her lips. Nicky, in his, stands ramrod straight in his school uniform and smiles the way boys do when they have been told to—that is, with a rigid, teeth-baring grin. The picture makes August laugh.

"He can smile naturally when no one is paying attention," Etna says. "But somehow he thinks more is expected of him when his picture is being taken."

"Your daughter is lovely," August says. "I see a lot of you in her. The mouth, the chin."

"Yes, she has begun to look more and more like me, despite the contrast in our coloring."

"Your son will lose his extra weight when he reaches puberty," August reassures her.

"I fear he may have inherited his father's build."

"He's your child as well," August points out. "I expect him to be quite tall. Does he have large feet?"

"Yes," she says. "Too big for his body."

"There's your proof, then. He'll grow into his feet."

"What a funny concept."

"True, nevertheless. You're very lucky, Etna."

"Yes, I know. Now that Clara has moved north, it's much easier to be together. She and I have become quite close. I see her every week."

Etna describes her useless sessions with Dr. Little.

"I've made an appointment for you to visit Richard Parkhurst the day after tomorrow," August explains. "When I heard you would be here for such a short stay, he and I agreed that there was no time to lose."

"I know that the 'cure' to my last ailment lies here, not in America. If it did lie there, I am certain I would be done with it. In fact, during the last several months, the pains in my legs have increased in frequency, not decreased."

"I once learned not to dismiss your hunches."

Etna laughs.

"You're the same and not the same," he says.

"I was someone else. Do you ever think about her?"

"Yes, I do. Often."

"Tell me about you."

He sets his teacup down. "Well," he says, picking off an imaginary piece of lint from his trousers, "I'm in the midst of changing professions. Now that the war is over, there is, happily, less demand for cranial surgery. I'm reading psychiatry, which can't be a complete surprise to you."

"I'm pleased for you," she says.

"Would you like to see the orangery?" he asks. "For old times' sake?"

"I would love to," she says.

From the glass dome, Etna peers down into the tall bare trees, wet now with the midday sun. She inspects the rooftops and chimney pots, faintly pink from the low angle of the light this time of year. Inside the glass dome, there are no blossoms on the trees and certainly no fruit. But the life in them is apparent. The soil feels rich to Etna's touch.

She circumnavigates the dome, touching bark and leaves as she goes. "What did we do here?" she asks.

August, already seated, seems surprised by the question. "Your memories came as small jolts," he says.

"And then I had one big jolt."

"I would have said that you were catapulted into yourself by your spoken name."

"Do you think," Etna asks, "that on that first day, the day you found me in the garden, if I'd heard my real name, I'd have accepted it?"

"Yes, but the shock—and I hesitate to use the word; it's imprecise—might have been too much for you."

"I was happy here," she says.

"But you struggled."

"I was happy here," she repeats. "You drew out my artistic skills."

"Merely encouraged them. In retrospect, the best I can say for what happened here is that I helped you to prepare yourself for the moment you would discover who you were. As you wrote to me, your drawings were in fact memories trying to break through. As for the rest, other circumstances proved more efficacious. Really, the most important thing you did here was to unburden yourself of poisonous images."

"I suppose I have worked out that the deafness I experienced when I saw children in the garden here and other places represented an inability to tolerate my feelings of guilt at having abandoned my children. So that when I saw children, I went deaf to prevent myself from hearing their cries—by that I mean my imaginings of their cries."

"And then once you had gone deaf, you were able to sink into a kind of calming joy," August says.

"Yes," Etna says.

"That would seem to make sense."

"And I'm positive, as I wrote you, that the menace I felt at the back of my neck that manifested itself in a kind of seizure ended the moment I had the courage to drive past the house where Van Tassel and I lived as man and wife. The sense of menace was because I feared him—both emotionally and physically."

"Do you still fear him?"

"No," she answers honestly. "I don't."

There is a silence between them.

"August, I must see Phillip."

"Phillip Asher?"

She knew that August would be curious, hearing the name. But she did not expect him to look so surprised.

"I have never met him," August says.

"I haven't seen him since that moment in the hospital tent

when he was brought in with his damaged face. I've written to him at the convalescent hospital in Kent where he is staying but have had no reply."

August clears his throat. "I can't encourage you to pay a visit to Phillip Asher. The sight of him may once again be too painful for you. But I understand that if you've come all this way for that purpose, no one can dissuade you. I can arrange for the appointment. I'd be more than happy to go with you. By the way, where are you staying?"

Etna names the hotel.

"When would you like to make the visit?" he asks. "Normal procedure in such a circumstance is to call and ask for an appointment, particularly with severe cases. We don't want to visit when Asher is recovering from a recent surgery, for example."

And Etna can see that during those practical sentences, August has recovered himself.

"Can you take care of that?" she asks.

"Yes, I will. When we go downstairs."

"The crossing was awful. The sea was roiling."

"After so much death on the sea from German torpedoes, it's easy to forget that the ocean itself is man's most dangerous threat. Were you frightened?"

"One gets tired of being frightened, wouldn't you agree?"

"Yes, I would."

"I must go home with a letter from Parkhurst. August, I dislike using you in this way."

"You don't use me. You have never *used* me. I had hoped we had gotten beyond the doctor-patient bargain we made so long ago."

"We have," she says.

\*    \*    \*

August follows Etna down the several flights of stairs and has her wait with him in the morning room while he telephones the director of the convalescent hospital. He asks about visiting Phillip Asher. It is the director's opinion that Phillip might well benefit from company. He has few visitors.

"We can go as soon as next week," August says to Etna when he has hung up.

"Then yes, let's do that. I need no preparation."

"I think lunch is ready."

"I was hoping you would show me around London a bit, if you have the time."

"I shall make the time," August says, smiling. "I'll come round for you at your hotel tomorrow morning, say around eleven?"

"Perfect," she says.

Etna tucks her hand into the crook of August's elbow. They have had their luncheon on the Strand and now stroll toward Covent Garden. They have no destination, a state Etna prefers more than any other. Their height causes passersby to glance in their direction.

"When I arrived in Camiers," she says, "I asked everyone I knew if he or she had ever met a man named Phillip Asher, ambulance driver. For months, I had no response. But then one day he came to my tent. It seemed improbable, after what he had been through in America, and what he experienced in France, that he looked so normal, so willing to engage in life. I may have written to you about some of this."

"Yes."

"In a moment of madness, I had gone to France. My children were in America. I was working in hellish circumstances. But Phillip's face, when I first saw it in my tent, was very welcome."

"Do you really think you were mad, clinically speaking, when you fled?"

"I do. Maybe others would call it a nervous breakdown, an inability to function in reality, to reason. Who would choose to go to the most dangerous place on earth?"

The air is frigid, painful. August wears a hat and muffler. Etna has the collar of her wool coat up around her ears.

"Do you think you unconsciously wanted to commit suicide?" he asks.

"By erasing Etna and becoming Stella? The thought has occurred to me."

Tomorrow August will have her driven to Richard Parkhurst's office. They have both agreed that Etna's chances for a satisfactory outcome, one that will persuade the judge, are better if August is not involved from this point on. On Thursday night, she will go with August to the theater, and they will have a light supper afterward. On Friday morning, they will drive to Kent to see Phillip.

"What did Phillip say when you first spoke with him?" August asks.

"I told him I wanted him to go back with me to America so that Clara would have a chance to recant her accusation, thus allowing him to regain his reputation. But he brushed the offer away. He didn't live in the past. He had somehow learned to live in the present. We had fun together. We went dancing one night, played tennis one afternoon. Simple, normal activities took on heightened significance, a way of defying all that was around us. A glass of wine at a café was festive."

August is silent.

"We weren't lovers," Etna quickly adds, and she can feel August's relief in his arm. "If you had been there, you would have understood how it was."

"I very much wanted to go," he reminds her.

"Be so glad that you didn't. No man could have done more for the war effort than you. I was a witness. I saw."

"I wonder."

"You're very dear to me, August. I would hate to think you were somehow disappointed in yourself."

Approaching another strolling couple—so young, Etna thinks—she and August move to one side.

"So you see, when I saw Phillip that last time, with his face horribly disfigured, I believe I went mad again. I remember running into a field. After that, I have no memory until I woke at Marne. I think it likely I'll never know how I got from Camiers to Marne."

"You had to have been driven," August reasons.

"The head sister at Marne said I was brought in on a cart. She didn't know by whom." Etna imagines herself being driven to Marne in a midnight-blue touring car. They enter a sparkling garden. "London is full of these, isn't it?" she asks, meaning small parks.

"It's what makes London so easy to walk through. Fortunately most of the gardens in the city are not locked. Just when you start to feel weary, there's a tucked-away patch of grass and a bench."

"Do you want to be a psychiatrist?" she asks.

"I believe in talk therapy. I've come to believe in the good it does."

"Did I start that? Did our time together lead to this?"

"Yes, I think so."

They sit together on a dry stone bench.

"Were you an artist before you became Stella Bain?"

"I drew as a child the way other girls played the piano or crocheted. It was a suitable occupation for a young woman, but nothing more. With little encouragement, it seemed pointless to continue, although I did do some floral studies while I was at the cottage."

"How amazing that your talent blossomed with Stella and made you so happy."

"And a good thing, too. Otherwise I don't know how I'd be able to make a living now. The money allows me to live an independent life."

"Wouldn't you rather be happily married?"

"I can't begin to answer that," she says. "I can't connect the word *happy* with marriage."

"Your desire for independence has always fascinated me."

"But should it, really? If I were a man, you wouldn't give it a second thought."

"I might give it a second thought, but not a third. Marriage is the norm."

A whole generation is missing its men, she thinks. Will all the "norms" change now?

August puts his hands on his thighs. "Shall we see the Tower or get a cup of tea?"

"I think the tea," she says.

They do not speak much on the drive to Kent. August and Etna sit in the back while Dodsworth, Mary's husband, drives. Etna is relieved that he came home from the war safely; perhaps he and Mary have already had a child. She tries to focus on the visit to come. While she is afraid of having to look at Phillip, she knows she needs to see him, to reassure herself that his spirit, at least, is intact.

The stillness between her and August feels much the same as on the first day they went to the Admiralty together.

The Austin moves smartly up to the front door of the convalescent hospital. August helps Etna from the motorcar. It is even colder in the country than in the city, and a fresh breeze stings.

"Meet us back here in two hours," August instructs Dodsworth.

Etna takes in the well-manicured surroundings. The stones of the building still hold their golden warmth in the pale light, and one cannot help but be impressed. She guesses the "tuition" at this institution to be quite a sum, and she has to remind herself that the estate is a laboratory for physicians as well as a residence for soldiers who have lost their faces in the war.

"What a gracious building," she says to August.

"Keep in mind that the sights we're about to see will be difficult at best," he warns.

"You seem to have forgotten that I saw many 'difficult' sights during my time in France."

"Yes, and one of them caused you to lose your memory."

It is as if they have stepped into the great hall of a well-tended manor house. Indeed, they are hard-pressed to find an artifact or person who looks even vaguely official. Etna spots a small sign displaying an arrow and the word *Visitors*. She imagines that parents and wives find the grand but welcoming surroundings comforting, as if the man they are about to leave here will be spending a holiday at a country house.

August and Etna locate a well-dressed middle-aged woman who asks if they want tea while they wait for the director to be free. They refuse politely, but the woman (nurse; assistant; receptionist?) insists on taking their coats. She explains that having outerwear on suggests to patients too brief a visit and often makes them anxious. Thus Etna and August enter the pageant that is being played out this day.

The director receives them in good time, and they are led into a space that might be an office but appears to be a gentleman's library. The room, Etna has no doubt, exists as a place to greet family members and donors, not a place to see the injured.

"We have the capability of caring for sixty patients," the director says. "We have a staff of eight doctors and over twenty nurses, all of whom live on the premises. Often a single case demands the skills of several surgeons: one to repair a shattered palate, one to build a new jaw, one for bone transplanting, and one to see to the skin grafting and the insertion of wax beneath the skin to make the visage more lifelike. The hospital also has several artists whose sole occupation is to develop templates for tin masks and paint them. A surgeon can repair a bludgeoned face, but an artist is needed to render an aesthetically pleasing result."

He consults a daily time sheet. "Phillip Asher is with a visitor now," he informs Etna and August.

"Who is the visitor?" August asks, much surprised.

"Captain Samuel Asher, Phillip's brother. He arrived unexpectedly an hour ago to say good-bye to his brother. I gather he is returning to Canada."

For a time, neither August nor Etna speaks. How can she interrupt what may be a last visit between the brothers for some time to come?

"You have traveled so far," August offers.

"Perhaps we could simply interrupt Captain Asher's visit, and then he can resume when we leave," Etna suggests.

"Yes; we can hardly go back to London now."

"If you are agreed . . ." says the director.

"We are."

Etna and August are ushered into a large common room in which men sit in wheelchairs or at tables while others stroll back and forth in front of a massive fireplace. Faces hide, half shrouded in their tin masks. Other visages are in various states of preparation. Etna knows that an expression of normalcy on her part is essential.

Four men sit at a table playing cards. Several more read in rocking chairs. The hush seems strange to Etna. She supposes the patients knocking metal trays to the floor are elsewhere.

A man with thinning red hair raises his arm. In his military uniform, Samuel stands at their approach, but Phillip, with his tin-and-enameled mask, remains seated.

"So surprised to see you both," Samuel says. "But I'm delighted. Etna, when did you arrive?" Samuel shakes hands with August. Across the expanse of a table and two chairs, she meets the captain's eye. His coloring seems to have faded since she saw him last, as if the war itself had kept him young. She wonders what sort of a home and family he will go to now.

Etna lowers herself into a chair near Phillip's. Samuel seems excessively buoyant, perhaps trying to make up for Phillip's rude stare. Etna senses that Phillip feels himself to be a grotesque attraction, such as one might find at a village fair.

There are two halves to his face, one flesh and the other made of tin overlaid with enamel paint. The shadow of the mask on the real face causes a dark line to bisect the visage. The expressions on the two sides of the face are at odds with each other, the false side, paradoxically, the more lively looking. Etna imagines that when Phillip sat for his portrait, he was in a considerably better mood than he is now. Either that or the artist wished a better mood upon him, believing that seeing the good spirits on the one side would create them on the other. Phillip's working eye is alert but wary, and it takes all of Etna's concentration not to reach over and touch him.

Samuel and August do much of the talking, as if they are the adults and Etna and Phillip but tongue-tied children. Etna thinks the scenario perverse.

"Mr. Asher," August asks of Phillip, "do you like it here? Your surroundings are quite beautiful."

Etna watches for any signs of a response. At first she thinks August will have none, but then Phillip casts his good eye in the doctor's direction. "I'm sorry, but do I know you?"

Etna realizes that in the initial confusion, Samuel did not introduce August to his brother.

"My apologies," August says, half rising. "I'm August Bridge, a friend of Etna's." The ways in which he knows Etna are too complicated to explain. Etna notes that August did not add the honorific Doctor, doubtless because he did not want Phillip to think he was under observation.

Etna leans forward in Phillip's direction. She reaches her hand toward him and then withdraws it. "Phillip," she finally whispers.

He turns to her.

She scans his face without flinching. She studies the surgeries she can see.

Her legs begin to tingle. *God, no.* She holds her breath. She cannot have an episode here—not in front of Phillip, who will think the sight of his face has brought on her distress.

Her hands go to her calves. *Not now,* she pleads.

She should excuse herself immediately before the pains come on full. She waits a minute, both Samuel and Phillip perplexed, while her palms remain where she has placed them.

She waits another minute.

When Etna lets her hands go, they drift upward, as if weightless.

A waiter appears with a tray. The business with the tea covers Etna's physical relief.

She notices on the tray a glass of tea with a straw. The extent to which Phillip's life has been diminished dismays her, she who should have been prepared for anything. But she has never been required to imagine what such a life would be like, minute by boring minute.

In London, Etna saw men with similar masks, and somehow, though she always noticed, they failed to provoke the reaction she is having now. What upsets her, she thinks, is the contrast between Phillip's beauty, more than evident in the half of him that is real, with the ugliness of the replica. Phillip must see that contrast each morning in the mirror, which he has to use to adjust the mask. Some of the men, Etna has noticed, wear spectacles to keep the masks in place, one side of the spectacles embedded into the tin.

Does Etna take milk and sugar? Milk, but not the sugar, she answers Samuel. August, the opposite. Samuel, black. As Etna is handed her cup, she wants to scream. For Phillip, who seems to want nothing more than to be left alone. For herself, who has come to see the man who was so badly hurt. For August, who seems deeply saddened.

"I must speak to Phillip alone," Etna announces in a low voice.

"Are you sure?" Samuel asks after a few seconds pass.

"If you don't mind, I'd like both of you to wait for me elsewhere."

"Etna has come a long way to speak to your brother," August gently reminds Samuel.

"Yes, of course," Samuel says.

August turns to the man with the half mask. "Good-bye, Phillip," he says. "It was a pleasure to meet you, and I wish you well."

August stands. Samuel tells Phillip that he will be back.

When the men are gone, Etna adjusts her chair and moves the table a bit so that she is sitting across from Phillip. "I've been in America gathering my children."

"Samuel says you lost your memory."

"I thought my name was Stella Bain."

"I'm happy for you that you have your children back."

"Your face is very beautiful," she says, gazing at his handsome features.

"Etna," he says with a laugh. "You were ever the optimist."

"As I recall it, *you* were the optimist."

"Maybe I was."

"Has it been very terrible?" she asks.

"What, nine surgeries? Nothing to it."

"Phillip."

They are close to each other, knees to knees. She bends her head and lays her arms along his. She remains in that position—a supplicant? A penitent? A restless spirit wanting comfort?—until he raises her up.

"Etna," he says, "you're stronger than this."

"Am I?"

"The pain has been difficult to deal with. There's no point in pretending it hasn't. But after the first several months, I became, in an odd way, accustomed to life here. It's not without its pleasures."

Etna cannot imagine what they are. "Do you have friends?" she asks.

"I do," he says. He pauses. "There's something I want to tell you."

"Of course."

"Etna, I have someone."

"Here?"

"Yes. A patient like myself."

It takes Etna a few seconds to understand what Phillip is trying to tell her. And then she thinks, of course. Phillip collected beautiful things. He said he had once known love. He spoke of a beautiful man. Earlier, in America, he invented a fiancée. But mostly, it was in the way he was with Etna in France. He loved her, she knew, but without urgency.

She covers his hand. "I'm glad for you," she says. "What's his name?"

"William. I sometimes see on his face the same expression I once saw on yours so many years ago."

The actual name impresses the reality upon her. She knows nothing of this kind of love.

"Did you guess?" he asks.

"No, but some things make sense now."

"I once tried to tell you."

"Do you still collect beautiful things?" she asks.

"I can't," he says. "There are too many of them here. Ruins the game."

She laughs.

"Are *you* happy, Etna?"

"Yes, I think so. Yes, I am. I am so much better off than when I knew you in France."

"When do you leave?"

"Soon."

A shadow crosses his face. "But time enough for another visit?" he asks.

"Do you want me to come?"

"Of course I want you. I'm desperate for a fourth for bridge. William doesn't play."

\*    \*    \*

"I'm sorry," August says when Etna finds him in the lobby.

"He says he is content. He may even be happy."

August shakes his head, bewildered.

"I felt sad for him, but he wasn't sad," she adds.

"At least there's that."

"It was important for me to visit him," she explains.

"I didn't understand until I saw the two of you together."

Etna tilts her head. "How do you mean?"

"I mean I understand now why you have to be with him."

Etna narrows her eyes. "You think I came to England for Phillip," she says.

August stands perfectly still.

"I came to get *you*," she whispers.

"I'm sorry?"

"You, August. I came to get you."

"Etna, you surprise me," he says.

"Are you really surprised?"

"My God." He takes her hand and leads her along the corridor until he finds an empty room, well furnished, but of uncertain purpose. He embraces her and then pulls away to gaze at her. He draws her close and kisses her.

"After you left the Admiralty on the day Samuel said your name, I stumbled out of the building," he says. "I dismissed Mary Dodsworth and decided to walk home in the rain. I couldn't go to my clinic, and I certainly couldn't go home to Lily. I especially could not do that." He brings Etna to a pair of chairs near a window. When they sit, he leans toward her. "I was having trouble reconciling Stella with Etna. It seemed that

Stella had died, which felt like a true death. And she did die, she did. But what hurt so deeply was that I would never know Etna. Never know her life, who she had been, who she would become. It was impossible to believe that I had lost two women in a matter of seconds in the Admiralty. I knew objectively the two women were one and the same, but that wasn't how it felt. I understood that I knew Stella in a way no one ever would, and that despite my circumstances I had loved her. And now she had ceased to exist. I wandered in the rain, entered a pub, drank too much, went out again, and just walked. After a while, I found myself in one of those little gardens we were talking about. There was one iron bench, and I sat on it. And I wept."

"August," she says as she embraces him, pressing the side of her face into his. "I had no idea."

For a moment, they are silent.

"When did you know you had feelings for me?" Etna asks.

"When I woke you from the nightmare. I told myself that what I felt was merely a desire to protect you, but we never had another meeting when I wasn't aware of your exact physical proximity. When did you know?"

"When you asked me to draw my face. I remember I couldn't, and I lay my head against the couch, and I thought you would kiss my neck. I wanted you to." She puts her hand on August's woolen sleeve. "We have time now to talk about these things," she says, and as she does, a surge of feeling, not measured, not prepared for, travels from the center of her body to her mind—her own now, not injured, but rather bathed in the anticipation of a future with the man sitting so close to her.

\*     \*     \*

"It's unimaginable that Phillip should find love in such a place," August says as they are leaving the building arm in arm. "Oh, Lord."

"What?"

"The irony that Van Tassel should accuse Phillip of that particular crime!" August says with his free hand to his forehead.

"And Phillip couldn't use the one thing that would exonerate him."

"It's a travesty."

They walk together in silence.

"The pains in my legs threatened to come, but didn't," Etna tells him.

"I wondered about that. They didn't come at all?"

"No. I was so relieved."

"Has this ever happened to you before, that you thought they were coming, but they didn't?"

"No."

"Then perhaps they are gone?"

"I don't know. Do you think, August, that the pains came because I ran away from Phillip? When I saw his injured face?"

"Possibly. But I think it's probably more complicated than that. It seems more likely that they came because you *couldn't* run away."

"From Marne?"

"I'm thinking of your husband. You couldn't run away for so many years, and then you did. From him, but also from your children. For which you must have had deep unconscious guilt when you were in Marne."

"And then I ran from Phillip."

"Yes."

"Which was why I knew I had to see him again?" Etna asks.

"My God, Etna. I can hardly think," he says, his voice full of emotion. "You and Parkhurst will have to work that out."

The Austin speeds through a frosted countryside.

Etna reaches for August's hand. She entwines her fingers and presses hard against his. He returns the pressure.

"I must go back," Etna says. "I have to be with my children."

"Would it be wrong of me to point out that there are schools in America where I can pursue my studies?" August asks, and she can hear the edge of excitement in his voice, an excitement she shares.

"It wouldn't be wrong of you."

"Etna, I have never been this happy."

Despite Dodsworth's presence up front, August kisses Etna, an awkward kiss with coats and hats and spectacles. When they break away, she laughs.

"Just wait until I get you alone," he whispers.

She will not ask if he ever felt this way with Lily. That knowledge is not hers to have. It is enough—it is so much more than enough—that he is with her now.

He will be her one-room cottage, her oasis.

*The Coast of New Hampshire, 1930*

How strange this happiness, the pain of it. Aware of minutes, she remembers years. She would remember every hour if she could. To live a life and then recall that life in equal time. What a thought! She wishes it could be done.

She slips off her smock, walks through the bedroom, and stands at the window. The water-sparkle blinds her. The sun just right, the tide moving at a rapid clip, a perfect June day. After lunch they will meander along the village lane and then walk out to the point where a house, vacant and abandoned, decomposes in the sea salt.

He has gone out for lobster but will return soon. She imagines him as he enters a shop she has been in a hundred times. He will take off his hat, and his hair will be creased in the back. He will raise a hand—that familiar gesture—and smooth the crown, missing the crease.

Sometimes she can see the scoliosis, one shoulder slightly higher than the other.

He will make a pleasantry, perhaps even a joke. He will twirl his hat on his finger. Henry Benedict, grocer, his large red hands planted squarely on the scarred wooden counter, will ask after her.

\*　　\*　　\*

She opens the window and lets in the smell of fast-running seawater and sun-warmed stones. The shingled cottage is modest, the rooms small territories reclaimed in battle, the memory of that earlier cottage not as keenly felt, which makes memory possible.

When he returns from the grocer's, he will touch her shoulder or her neck. He will talk to her of Henry Benedict, who writes his sums on a paper bag, whose shirt beneath the bloodstained apron is always beautifully pressed. Mrs. Benedict sews and irons behind a bombazine curtain, which occasionally emits a sullen boy, the son, carrying tinned peas or bananas.

Etna craves a banana now. She can taste the texture of the fruit, the gelatinous sweetness on the tongue. She will not ask August to go out again, though it is an errand he would gladly do.

Behind her stands the mahogany bed they purchased together in Boston. She has linen curtains at the windows, a Turkish carpet on the floor. Wallpaper covers the worn plaster.

Through the window, she can see the entire tide pool. The shifting shades of blue; the sea-grass green; no tinge of russet yet. The dock is big enough for a man's fishing boat. Beside the cottage are others like it, and then the Benedicts'. Beyond that, the sea. In the afternoons, she has to hold her hand against the white sheet that is the ocean.

He will come in bareheaded, having removed his coat and hat downstairs. Perhaps his face will be pink with the fine weather and his exertion. He will tell her of how he met Stringfellow on his way home and how they talked of fishing. He will remember that Benedict asked after her.

On the dressing table, there are cut-glass jars of scents and pins. A knitted throw lies folded at the bottom of the chaise longue. She remembers yarn through her fingers, the pleasant surprise of cloth made from string. Of art made with a pencil. Her pictures now consist of oil paint on perfectly smooth canvas, the paintings as austere as architectural drawings, overpainted with less restrained splashes and lines of color. Blood red for field hospitals, blue for men who stand by iron gates in winter. Her love of color, the mixes, until the right shade of mauve or straw is achieved. The tension between the formality of the drawings and the release of color, the art. A different color each painting, bringing out a thought that might be missed.

He has put the two catalogs of her shows on her nightstand so that she might, if she wishes, peruse a life's work. But *he* is her life's work, she tries to tell him. *Her children* are her life's work. *She* is her life's work.

Clara will come soon with her girls. And Nicky, too, newly graduated from Dartmouth. And Sebastian, thirteen now, about to enter Exeter, the place where Etna's father and Samuel used to teach. Sebastian is with them always, just off now with friends, learning how to sail.

After a visit with his father, Nicky will spend the summer with Etna and August on his way to Boston for law school. Etna never asks about his father, but she sometimes wonders if Van Tassel, who granted her a divorce in 1920, bemoans the loss of his family, which he abandoned as much as she. Or is he complacent, content to sit at his desk in his study in his home in Thrupp, pondering whom to hire and whom to fire?

Clara is a beauty, as predicted, her coloring fair, her lips full, her eyes, when suddenly presented, a surprise. She and her husband, Ned, live in Boston, his insurance company riding out the economic collapse.

In 1919, Etna was granted custody of Nicky on the condition that she would enter him in private school when he turned fourteen and that she would take him to church every Sunday. August loved the boy, and the boy in turn learned to love the man.

When was it she first moved to this seaside village? Eight years ago? She moved for the light, yes, but also to have a home for her family—this one not a secret, but hers nevertheless, bought with the labor of her hands.

She has always liked her windows clean. More often than not she climbs the ladder herself, learning to balance, newsprint in one hand, vinegar in the other. For this she has made a spectacle of herself. She is known as house-proud, a mantle she does not mind shouldering. Clarity is worth the sacrifice.

August will come soon. She knows this. He keeps a boat in the tide pool. They take it out for picnics.

\*        \*        \*

Etna remembers her visit to the convalescent home in Kent in the winter of 1919. Samuel with his brotherly concern, Phillip with his secret, August with his bewilderment, and she with her guilt, finally assuaged that day. She held Phillip's arms and bent her head and wanted to stay in that position for the rest of her life. But then Phillip lifted her up. She saw his living face as a beautiful thing. It showed a man who knew love. The tin mask was a caricature of life: they had painted a half mustache; the color of the eye was off.

Phillip lives on Beacon Hill. He has a town house he bought with his share of the family money. A man he loves, perhaps not the same man as before, has elegant rooms nearby. Phillip is a poet of some repute and is not afraid to go about in public, the surgeries having repaired more of the damage. She and August visit him from time to time when they are in Boston. Because of the scar tissue, Phillip looks exceptionally pale and perhaps unwell, and he wears dark glasses and a hat, and possibly you might not want to introduce yourself to him. But you could not say for certain, in the shade, that he had been damaged by the war.

When she stands before the God she has renounced, this will be her greatest sin, not to have known that Clara was lying. A lie that set in motion Phillip Asher's demise. The man humiliated, twice ruined, once in Thrupp, and then on a field in France. And yet somehow thriving despite it all.

After the visit to the convalescent home, she rode back with August to his house. Once inside the door, with Streeter discreetly dismissed and the nanny upstairs with Sebastian for his nap, August kissed her again and again. Each had waited for the other for so long. She remembers that a carillon was ringing from a church tower. That night, in her old bed, the one she had when she was a guest in that house, his body was persuasive, and she discovered again the joys of the erotic life. He was an inventive lover, always tender.

She pinches her cheeks and wets her lips. She can see him coming down the lane. She listens for his footsteps on the narrow stairway.

"Etna," he says, as if she were new to him.

She sees, in quick succession, a smile, a perspiring brow. He comes to where she stands by the window and rests an elbow on the wooden rail. He wears a shirt with the sleeves rolled, the tie loosened, the collar open but not removed.

"You have on your dark glasses," she says.

"Do I?" he asks, pulling them off his face. He studies them as if alchemy has been involved. He takes his clear spectacles from his pocket. But she has seen him naked, with the lost look of the myopic.

"Are you feeling all right?" she asks. "You're perspiring somewhat." She touches his brow.

"Maybe a little tired is all."

She had a bout of the flu the previous winter, and it weakened her—her lungs never very strong after that first collapse in Bryanston Square. They are shortly to travel to London with Sebastian for their annual visit so that he may see his relatives. August will deliver a series of lectures at the British Psychoanalytic Society.

*   *   *

Her heart is wild and loose inside her chest.

"Are *you* feverish?" he asks, misunderstanding.

"No, I'm perfect," she answers and laughs.

"Do you remember everything?" she asks.

"Every moment, no."

"I wish I could. How long can you stay this time?"

"Until Tuesday, anyway."

"What about the patients?"

"The Monday patients have been rescheduled."

August, too, has a set of rooms on Beacon Hill, one of which he uses as an office. Streeter, who still attends to August when he is in the city, gambles on the horses and seems, despite the odds, to have made a small fortune for himself.

"Did I tell you that I have a patient with intractable shell shock? The man was nineteen when he went to war. He's thirty-two now. He can't stop cowering at any loud noise. He's woken up screaming from the same horrifying dream for twelve years. His wife is beside herself. She keeps asking, 'How long? How long?'"

"Don't give up on him," Etna pleads.

She remembers her own affliction, now immortalized in August's monograph on her case, the one he wrote after completing his training in psychiatry. To think of herself still wandering the earth, unaware that she has children. She cannot bear to imagine.

*   *   *

"How long before the last soldier of the Great War is dead?" she muses.

"Theoretically?" August peers out the window. "Well, if the boy got to France just under the wire in 1918, when he was seventeen, and he lived to be ninety-five, say..." He pauses. "His last Remembrance Day would be November eleventh, 1996. If he lived to be a hundred, it would be November eleventh, 2001."

"Unthinkable!" she exclaims.

"Unthinkable."

"They'd put him at the head of the parade."

"I should hope so."

"What's the news from Benedict?" she asks.

"Benedict?"

She smoothes the skirt of her dress. "Any news?"

"A family from Virginia is building a house just beyond his."

"On the hill?"

"If you can call it that."

"Does Benedict mind?"

"No. I rather think he likes it. More business. There will be carpenters and so forth. Men to feed."

"Is it to be a summer place?" she asks. "For the family?"

"I think so, yes."

She leans her head against his shoulder. He encircles her waist with his arms. What is it, after all, that she has done with her life? She had children and found them again. She fell in love at nineteen and again at forty-two. She tried to be an independent woman. She has earned her living by making pictures, some that disturb, some that please.

"Are you ready to go down?" he asks. "The lobsters await. Benedict's wife cooked them up. They're still hot in the paper bag. We'll eat on the back porch?" He kisses her hair.

She remembers the day they married. They stood by the sea in front of the cottage, only family in attendance to hear their private words. August gave her an emerald ring, and afterward they drove to Portsmouth for a celebratory lunch. They drank Champagne and devoured oysters and stayed until nearly teatime.

# Acknowledgments

My enormous thanks to Asya Muchnick, whose lovely demeanor and skill have been a joy to me; to Jennifer Rudolph Walsh, my kind, funny, and razor-sharp agent, who is *always* there when I need her; to Michael Pietsch, good friend and editor, who has been with me for nearly two decades of writing novels; to Caroline MacDonald-Haig, a London Blue Badge guide with tremendous knowledge of London, who shepherded me through that city; to Ivor Braka, who was kind enough to let me see the interior of his London house; to Lucie Dean, friend and enthusiastic guide, whose idea of "research" in London so closely matched my own—a necessary visit to the Imperial War Museum followed immediately by a trip to Harrods; to Katherine Clemans and Amy Van Arsdale, who both hold doctorates in psychology and who corrected mistakes in certain portions of the manuscript; to Richard Beswick, my British editor, who contributed a great deal to this book, both by pointing out Americanisms that would have been incorrect in British English and by giving me the idea of the trial; to Christopher Clemans, whose editorial acumen has recently been an inspiration to me; and to my good-natured husband, John Osborn, who silently put up with my moaning through all seven drafts of this novel and who is always ready to celebrate any good fortune that comes my way.

# About the Author

Anita Shreve is the acclaimed author of seventeen novels, including *Rescue; A Change in Altitude; Testimony; The Pilot's Wife,* which was a selection of Oprah's Book Club; and *The Weight of Water,* which was a finalist for England's Orange Prize. She was awarded the John P. Marquand Prize in American Literature. She lives in Massachusetts.

Reading Group Guide

*Stella Bain*

A NOVEL

by

ANITA SHREVE

# A conversation with Anita Shreve

*Stella Bain* tells the story of a severely shell-shocked American woman *who loses her memory after being found wounded on a French battlefield in 1916. A British surgeon, August Bridge, tries to help Stella recover her past and find her identity with a mixture of talk therapy and emotional support. How did the idea for this book emerge?*

I was interested in this period of history and also the idea of shell shock in women. I had read a lot about shell shock in men during World War I, but there wasn't a single diagnosis of shell shock in women. And that seemed incredible because they came under fire and were in the hospital tents, which were bombed, and they saw the worst that there was to see—men whose faces had been blown off, surgeons sawing limbs off and tossing them into buckets. And if they had what we would now recognize as shell shock, because they were women, they were termed hysterical and got no treatment whatsoever. So I was interested in exploring that and making Stella's life coincide with the life of a cranial surgeon who had a strong interest in what they called talk therapy then.

Also, my grandfather was in the First World War, and although he didn't talk much about it because we were just his grandchildren, it did have a fascination.

*How did you research the World War I battlefield experiences of women?*

I read a lot of books about it, but I also went to original sources to see just what equipment they had used. A lot of research also hinges on photographs. Sometimes you see a picture and that's really all you need for that little part of the story.

*It was also an interesting time in that women were just starting to express their independence and take on roles traditionally considered male. I wondered if you were trying to reflect that in Stella's character, because she seems quite empowered and determined.*

Well, by that time she's been through the mill. She may not consciously know it at the very beginning of the book, but certainly she comes to remember it, and having been in that kind of a situation, she is no longer like any other American woman she might know at the time. She's driven an ambulance, she's been under fire, she's gone through all the hospital experiences that I talked about, she's found herself in situations that she couldn't even have imagined. And I think once you have survived a hell like that, unless you're crushed altogether, you do come out intrinsically a stronger person even if that wasn't your goal in the first place.

*Where did the name Stella Bain come from?*

I can't really tell you that because it is an anagram of who she becomes. She's actually a character from another novel.

*Is that something that you try to do, interconnect your novels somehow?*

No, I don't try to do it. In fact, it's very awkward and a pain in the neck. Because I'd gone on and on about this woman, then I decided to reread the original book, and at the end there were all sorts of facts that didn't really work. So I had to tiptoe and change and do all sorts of things to make it plausible that one could happen. It was satisfying when I finished it, and anyone who's deeply familiar with both books—and I'm not going to name the other one right now—will say, "Ah, OK, so that's what happened to her."

*That's fascinating. I've heard you also like to slip mentions of things or clues into your books so regular readers will pick up on things that others less familiar with your work won't.*

I have four novels that take place in the same house in New Hampshire (the Fortune's Rocks quartet—*Fortune's Rocks, The Pilot's Wife, Sea Glass,* and *Body Surfing*), and if I began a novel that doesn't immediately tell you that, there will be a reference to a painting, and then a reader who knows my work will know that: "Ah, that painting was in such and such."

*In* Body Surfing *it seemed that you might be saying good-bye to the house in New Hampshire. Were you?*

I think not. I think that house has many lives I have not explored yet.

*In the acknowledgments you say you went through seven drafts of this book. Was that normal or did this book take longer?*

Oh no, seven is excessive, I think. And none of it was happy. I'd love to say I just loved writing this book and it was just such a pleasure, and parts of it were. But writing it seven times is not really my cup of tea. It took me a long time to figure out who should tell the story, from what point of view, should it be multiple points of view, should it be in the past tense, should it be in the present tense, what the structure should be. It's a complicated structure because you cannot do it chronologically without giving the end away, so I had to think about how that was going to work. There were a lot of "Well, if I do this, then that happens, so, OK, no, I can't do that, so how about if I try this?" It wasn't organic.

*I read that you attempt something new or different with every book. What were the new things you were taking on with this book?*

It was a different era, it was bolder, my canvas was bigger, and it wasn't entirely a love story; it had a much broader range.

*Many of your protagonists seem as if they're either besieged or maybe wronged in some way and have to embark on a difficult and vital quest—is that something you like to return to?*

I'm really interested in the catastrophic moment in life. If you push a woman to the edge, how will she behave? And the idea that there's a catastrophic moment or a moment that sets everything else in motion and you can sometimes see a definite before and after and how do you cope after that moment. But yes, I do, the struggle to return or to overcome or make things happen—and sometimes they don't, sometimes a catastrophe is a catastrophe, such as in *The Weight of Water*—there's no growing stronger after that one.

*Is there anything, emotionally speaking, that you wouldn't or couldn't write about?*

Well, I don't know. I killed off children; I think that's probably about as hard a thing to do as anything. I wouldn't write gory details or horror or magical realism or fantasy—and I'm highly unlikely to ever write a novel about zombies. I'm very interested in real people and how they behave and real circumstances.

# Reading Group Guide • 7

*Do you find you draw from real life, or once you've created a character, do you find you follow them and imagine exactly how they would respond to a given situation?*

Here's the thing—the characters get created through the process of writing, and sometimes they're not fully alive until quite a while into the book, and there's this moment where you say, "Oh wow, OK, so that's who that person is." And you write it and it seems to have absolutely nothing to do with you, and then later after it's published other people say, "Well, you realize who that was, don't you?" Or, "You realize what you were trying to do there?" It's hard to believe that a novelist could write a whole novel and not have a clue about what's really going on, but it has happened to me.

*Really? And what did you say when you were confronted with that?*

I was horrified, absolutely horrified. It was a particular situation where my mother was pointing out to me who all the different characters were, and I was stupefied and she was stupefied because she couldn't believe I didn't know this. She thought I was deliberately writing them out, and I'd been congratulating myself all along that here I'd gone and written one of my early novels and it didn't have anything to do with me, there was no place you could point to a connection. But, you know, a mother sees a different story.

*Which book was that?*

It was *Eden Close.*

*Do you feel she was right?*

Oh, yes. She was absolutely right.

*What's your typical writing day like? Do you write every day?*

I write every day that I don't have a hiatus, and there are more than you would think—travel, kids coming home for holidays, a birthday, or just the weekend. But generally speaking, in the dead of winter when there is nothing to do except work, I would get up and be at the desk by seven-thirty, eight o'clock, and I would leave around twelve-thirty p.m.

*Do you still write in your bathrobe?*

I do.

*And do you write by hand?*

I do, and it takes twice as long doing a book because you then have to transfer it onto the computer, and it's cumbersome. I have tried to write right onto the computer, and the results are terrible.

*Was it literally seven different versions written out in longhand?*

Yes. Think of any possibility you can imagine as a way to tell that novel, and I tried it.

*That's amazing. That must be thousands of pages.*

Yes, and it doesn't translate—there's no button you can push that says, "Put this all in the past tense." By the way, the person who invents that button will make millions and millions of dollars. I would buy a machine that has that button.

*You write without showing anyone anything until you finish. Who is the first person who reads your manuscript?*

My husband. And he is very good—he's what I call a big-picture editor. He will say, "You know, I really love it. I'm just wondering, do you need the first forty pages?" and the minute he says it, they're gone. You know when an editor has really homed in on something because you say to yourself, "I knew that. I didn't do anything about it, I let it go, but I knew that."

*The Pilot's Wife was an Oprah's Book Club selection. At the time, did you consider it a blessing or a curse?*

I thought it was a thrill, an absolute thrill. And we had five kids to put through college and whatnot. It was very exciting, and I had many more readers than I had before. And I already had a backlist that practically no one knew about, so that was helpful. I think later on it became, you know, once you're in Oprah's Book Club, you do kind of get labeled, and it's been hard to break out of that. But I have to say that I'm infinitely more grateful than I am worried.

*Which writers have you most enjoyed reading recently?*

I thought Colum McCann's *TransAtlantic* was fantastic.

*Do you ever feel pressure from all your fans who are waiting for a new book from you that you can't let them down, or you don't want them to wait too long?*

I didn't have any control over it. I would like to have been able to give them a book a year, but that's just not going to happen. I'll probably spend some time on Facebook someday describing exactly why this didn't appear for three years, but for now it's just enough to have finished it.

*So it doesn't get any easier every time you write a book?*

No, no, clearly not! This was the hardest one of all. And this is another thing I would just like to say: When you're a writer, you learn nothing. You learn nothing. The book you are working on is the hardest thing you've ever done; there are no shortcuts, there are no tricks. The example I use is that of an architect. I've written seventeen novels. An architect who has built seventeen buildings, you would expect him to know a lot about structure and walls and all that stuff. But there's nothing that translates when you start a new novel. And part of that is what makes it exciting, but it's like you're on a high wire and there's no safety net.

*Do you know what you're going to write about next?*

I do, but I don't ever tell.

This interview was conducted by Catherine Elsworth for Goodreads.com. Catherine is a freelance writer based in Los Angeles.

# Questions and topics for discussion

1. Though the main character wakes without memory, one of the first things she does is settle on the name "Stella Bain." Later, when she hears her real name spoken, it brings back a flood of recollections. What is so significant about one's name? Given that we rarely choose our own names, why do they feel so intrinsic to our identities?

2. Why does Lily Bridge invite Stella into her home? Do you think she would have done so if Stella were not in uniform, and dressed either more formally or more shabbily? Would you have done the same in Lily's place? Why or why not?

3. Dr. Bridge hopes talk therapy will help cure Stella of her many strange ailments. Why was this approach so unusual at the time? What role, if any, do their sessions play in helping Stella regain her memory?

4. Do you think the relationship between Stella and Dr. Bridge is appropriate given the circumstances under which they are working together? If not, at what point do you think they cross a line?

5. What are Stella's biggest frustrations with her memory loss? How do you think you would react to losing your memory? Might there be anything liberating about the experience?

6. Stella wonders, "Can a man possibly care for a woman who is not herself? A woman who, with any luck, might change into someone else? Can a woman who is not herself truly care for another?" (p. 70). Do you think memory is an inherent part of one's personality, or is a person's character stable even if her memory has been lost?

7. In the field hospital, the ward nurse orders Stella to perform a

procedure that will result in a man's death, "because the soldier will die before the day is over, the sister...can use the bed for a man worth saving" (p. 88). Stella believes that this is unethical. Do you agree? Why or why not?

8. A fellow ambulance driver at the front describes to Stella his quest to find beauty, which, he says, "keeps me from going mad" (p. 100) in such a terrible place and time. Do you think this is a worthwhile quest? How does it relate to Stella's talent for drawing and the way she employs it over the course of the book?

9. Do you think Stella was justified in leaving home as she did and volunteering to serve in France? Were her actions cowardly or brave? Do you feel she deserves a second chance at regaining the privileges of the life she left behind? Or did she forfeit them when she left?

10. In the novel Shreve shows how a diagnosis of shell shock is "deeply troublesome" to civilians who haven't been to war and raises doubts about the competency of the person experiencing its symptoms (p. 209). Do you think we have made sufficient progress since World War I in dealing with post-traumatic stress? Is there still a stigma attached to it?

11. The war puts Stella through great trauma but also gives her opportunities she might not otherwise have had. In what ways does the war affect Stella, especially once she regains her memory and tries to resume her old life? Do you think by the end of the book she is grateful to have had the experiences she did, or does she wish they had never happened?

12. How, if at all, did the book change your understanding of World War I? Did it shed any light on the experience of non-combatants like Stella and Dr. Bridge, who were nonetheless swept up in the events of the time?

# *Anita Shreve's suggested reading for fans of* Stella Bain

*The Regeneration Trilogy,* Pat Barker

*The Beauty and the Sorrow,* Peter Englund

*The Great War and Modern Memory,* Paul Fussell

*To End All Wars,* Adam Hochschild

*The Great Silence,* Juliet Nicolson

*The Roses of No Man's Land,* Lyn Macdonald

*Testament of Youth,* Vera Brittain

*The Guns of August,* Barbara W. Tuchman

*The Virago Book of Women and the Great War,*
edited by Joyce Marlow

# Look for these other novels by Anita Shreve

## Rescue

"From its opening car crash, Anita Shreve's *Rescue* is worth the ride....No one can create the beginning of a complex relationship like Shreve....This random encounter in the small hours of the morning leads into a story of hope and fear, of promises made and broken."
　　　　　　　　　　　　　　　—Brigitte Weeks, *Washington Post*

## A Change in Altitude

"Heart-pounding....An engrossing novel about adventure in Africa and a marriage in turmoil."
　　　　　　　　　　　　—Cynthia Dickison, *Minneapolis Star Tribune*

## Testimony

"Contrasting the sweetness of young love with the primal recklessness of lust, Shreve paints a chilling portrait of how bad decisions in brief moments can ruin lives."
　　　　　　　　　　　　　　　　　—Joanna Powell, *People*

## Body Surfing

"Shreve, with her serene style and impeccable prose, returns....Here, a young widow gets drawn into a rivalry between two adult brothers, with heartbreaking consequences."
　　　　　　　　　　　　　　　　　　　　—*The Atlantic*